Stories
to Tell in
Children's Church

STORIES TO TELL IN CHILDREN'S CHURCH

Velma B. Kiefer

BAKER BOOK HOUSE
Grand Rapids, Michigan

Formerly published under the title
Please Tell Me a Story

Paperback edition issued 1976

Library of Congress
Catalog Card Number: 66-18309

ISBN: 0-8010-5371-4

Eleventh printing, May 1992

Printed in the United States of America

Foreword

Wise parents and teachers recognize the value of stories for their children — stories that will assist them in forming right attitudes and relationships to God and men. Stories can enlighten and give new insights. They can be helpful in recognizing and solving the problems of daily life. They can be useful in depicting standards of Christian behavior. They can lead to greater appreciation of God's love and care, and encourage trust in Him. And they may lead to worship and positive action.

It is my hope that these brief stories will make a small contribution in some of these ways. May children who read or hear them profit and may God be honored.

With one or two exceptions, these stories appeared originally in the *Church Herald*, and I wish to thank Dr. Louis Benes for his permission to publish them in this form.

V.B.K.

Contents

Stories
to Tell in
Children's Church

1

Caterpillar Cows

Have you ever heard of caterpillar cows? No? Well, let me tell you about them. These tiny cows live in the pinewoods of southern Mexico. They are only this _____ long. And they are the larvae of a rare butterfly. Their keepers are ants — ants which are this _____ long. These ants live in nests tunneled out of wood and are called carpenter ants.

All day the carpenter ants keep the caterpillar cows in burrows with doors made of wee wads of mud. Each cow is guarded by several ants.

But when the sun has gone down the guardian-ants open the mud doors. They crawl out of the burrows. Quickly they climb the bushes where the caterpillars like to feed. Carefully they inspect every twig and leaf. They look to see if there are any enemy bugs that might hurt the caterpillars.

About 7:30 they let the caterpillars out of the burrows. The ants shepherd the caterpillars to the bushes. Up to the tops of the bushes the caterpillars climb. There they nibble leaves hungrily. While they nibble their sunset supper the ants drink theirs. They drink the honey-dew "milk" the caterpillar-cows give.

In the morning when the sky begins to get light, the ants herd the caterpillars down the bushes. Back into the burrows they crawl. They pull their mud doors shut again. For eighty-three days the caterpillars are kept and milked by the friendly ants. Then the caterpillars sprout orange-rimmed wings and fly away — beautiful butterflies.

Scientists tell us that these caterpillars can live only where there are carpenter ants to guard them. Left alone they would soon be eaten by bugs or birds. In the animal kingdom God planned that these ants and caterpillars should need and help each other.

And in God's wisdom He has planned and made people to need and help each other, too. We are to help one another. God's Word says, "No man lives to himself."

2

Paula's Enemy

Paula slipped into her sky-blue organdy dress. Mother tied the sash for her and brushed her silky hair until it was soft and shining. Paula was going to Vacation Bible School. She could scarcely wait to go. She twirled around on her toes. But suddenly she stopped. A little frown puckered her forehead.

"Mother, will you go with me to the church?"

"Why?"

" 'Cause I have to walk past Mike's house. And he's mean. Everytime I go by his house he does something mean. He calls me silly names. Or he pulls my sash. Or he sneaks up behind me and gives me a hard push. He makes me so cross. Yesterday he even threw a stick at me. If he does it again I'll just throw it back at him. I don't like him. He's my enemy."

Mother sat down slowly. "I won't need to go with you because someone else will — Jesus will." Mother paused. "You know, if you think Mike is your enemy, then there is something you must do for him. Jesus said, 'Love your enemy and pray for him. Pay back his meanness by doing something nice for him.'

"I tell you what. Right now before you go, why don't we pray for Mike? We will ask Jesus to keep him from being unkind. And we will ask Jesus, too, that He will help you to love Mike and pay him back in kindness."

Paula watched Mother fold her hands in her lap. She wasn't sure she felt like praying for Mike. But she knelt by

Mother and folded her hands, too. And they prayed. When they were finished Paula was glad. The cross feeling inside was gone.

"Now let's see, can you think of something kind to do for Mike?" asked Mother.

Paula slid one shoe back and forth over the rug. She stared at it and thought. Then she clapped her hands. "I know! I bet he'd like some of the cookies you baked last night."

"I'm sure he would," agreed Mother. Quickly she got a little plastic bag for Paula. Paula put six, plump round cookies into it and Mother tied it shut with a red ribbon.

The bag of cookies in her hand, Paula started down the walk. Before she knew it she was at Mike's house. And there he was sitting on the steps and scowling.

"Hi," called Paula and smiled at him. "Look, I brought you some cookies my Mother baked." She held the bag of cookies toward him.

Mike was so surprised he didn't know what to say. Without thinking he reached out and took the bag.

"Thanks," he mumbled.

"I'm going to Bible School," announced Paula. "Why don't you come with me? I bet you'd like it."

Mike shook his head.

"Well, ask your Mother if you can go tomorrow?" suggested Paula.

She hurried off to church and to a happy morning in Bible School.

As she skipped home at noon, she saw Mike playing with his dog. "Hi," she called.

"Hi," answered Mike. "Those cookies were real good." He looked ashamed. "I'm sorry I threw a stick at you and teased you."

14

"And I'm sorry I got cross," said Paula. "Let's be friends, shall we?"

"O.K.," grinned Mike cheerfully. "And my Mother says I may go to Bible School with you tomorrow."

"I'm glad!" said Paula and ran home to tell her Mother.

"Oh, Mother, we had the best time at Bible School. And you know what? Mike liked the cookies. He's sorry he was mean. And you know what else? I asked him to go to Bible School — and he's going! And besides Jesus put it in my heart to like him, just like we asked Him to."

3

Find My Name!

One morning many years ago a little English boy chuckled — right in the middle of family prayers! His brother and sister were surprised. And his mother and father were displeased.

"Why did you giggle?" asked his father sternly.

The little boy pointed at the bell-rope near the fireplace. "Because," he said, "I saw a mouse run up that rope and I thought,

"There was a mouse for want of stairs
Ran up a rope to say his prayers."

Father didn't say a word. He just reached for a stick. Then the little boy begged,

"Oh father, father, pity take
And I will no more verses make."

But the father was not displeased because his son wrote verses. No, he only wanted him not to watch mice and make rhymes while the family was talking with God. This little boy kept on making rhymes about many things he saw and thought.

One time when he was only seven years old he wrote the poem you see here. In it he used the letters of his name. Can you discover what his name was? Read the two verses through. Now look at the first letter of each line. Do you see it? If you don't, then draw a line from the little star above the poem to the one below.

★

I am a vile polluted lump of earth,
S o I've continued ever since my birth
A lthough Jehovah grace does daily give me,
A s sure this monster Satan will deceive me,
C ome therefore, Lord, from Satan's claws re-
    lieve me.

W ash me in Thy blood, O Christ,
A nd grace divine impart,
T hen search and try the corners of my heart,
T hat I in all things may be fit to do
S ervice to Thee, and sing Thy praises too.

★

You see, the letters at the beginning of the first five lines spell his first name, and the beginning letters of the next five lines spell his family name.

Do you think you could write a poem like that? I'm sure I couldn't. But Isaac was a very bright boy. When he was

17

four years old he began to learn Latin. At nine he studied Greek. And at ten he was learning French!

Young Isaac knew he needed the Lord Jesus to cleanse his heart from sin. And he trusted in Jesus and wanted others to believe in Him too. When he grew up he often put words together to make beautiful hymns about our Saviour. Sometimes in Sunday school and church you sing some of the hymns he wrote. I'm sure that you sing his happy hymn *"Joy to the World"* every Christmas, and *"When I Survey the Wondrous Cross"* before Easter.

Isaac became a very famous preacher. He wrote many, many hymns for boys and girls and for grown-ups to sing. In fact, he wrote so many that he is called the "Father of English hymns."

4

A Happy Birthday

"When you have a birthday, how does your family celebrate it?" asked Miss Baker, smiling at her Sunday school class.

Dick's hand was up first. "My mother makes my favorite kind of meal — you know, like hamburgers and french fries. Besides, she bakes me a cake and puts candles on it. Then everyone sings 'Happy Birthday' to me before I blow out the candles."

"We always decorate a chair with bows of pretty paper ribbon," explained Betsy. "Whoever has a birthday sits in the birthday chair. We put our gifts on the table in front of the birthday chair. And after we've eaten, the gifts are opened so everyone can see them. Then Daddy prays especially for the one whose birthday it is."

"At our house," said Tim, "We each do or make something for the one who has a birthday. On my birthday my big brother made me a special box for my collection of stones. My mother let me choose what I would like her to cook for dinner. And Dad took me to the city zoo 'cause he knew how much I like to go."

One after the other the children told how their families celebrated their birthdays. Then Miss Baker asked, "But why do your parents and brothers and sisters do all these things on your birthdays?"

"That's easy," answered Dick, "They want to make us happy."

Miss Baker nodded. "That's right, Dick. Because they love us they want to give us joy on our birthday. On Christmas God's family celebrates the most important birthday in the world — Jesus' birthday. And because we love Him we want to make Him happy, too, don't we? How do you think we can make Him happy on His birthday?"

The children thought quietly for a few moments. "I know," said Jenny. "We can all sing 'Happy Birthday' to Him. He would hear us and be glad."

"I think it would make Him happy if we would tell Him we love Him," suggested Betsy. "And if we would show we mean it by doing what He likes us to do."

"We could thank Him 'specially for being born so He could grow up and die for our sins," thought Tim aloud.

"How about if we give some of our money to help the missionaries tell people about Him?" asked Ken.

"Very good, boys and girls," agreed Miss Baker, looking pleased. "Do you remember a Bible verse in which Jesus tells us another way to make Him happy on His birthday and other days, too? . . . I am thinking of a verse we learned last month."

Seven rememberers thought hard. But none could think which verse Miss Baker meant.

"Remember, Jesus said, 'Inasmuch as ye have shown kindness to one of the least of these my brethren, ye have done it unto me.' In this verse Jesus is saying, 'Whatever you do to make the poorest or smallest of my children glad, I will count it as if you have done it for me. When you are kind to one of my children, you are being kind to me.' You see, if we visit one of His sick or sad children, or if we give food, clothing, or room to one of his poor children, it is as if we have done this to Him.

"Since Christmas is Jesus' birthday, we who love Him should not be busy thinking about what makes *us* happy. But we should think about *Him* and plan and do what will please *Him*."

5

When Missi Forgot

The merry, brown-skinned orphan children on Aniwa Island were hungry. For weeks missionary John Paton had had only a little food to give them.

"Missi," — for that is what the children called the missionary — "we are very hungry," they said one day.

"So am I," answered Mr. Paton. "But we will have little food until the supply ship brings us more."

"Oh, Missi," begged the hungry children. "You have two beautiful fig trees. May we eat their young, tender leaves? We'll be careful not to hurt the trees."

"Gladly, children. Help yourselves," smiled Mr. Paton.

Quickly the boys and girls scrambled up the trees. Like happy little squirrels they sat on the branches and ate.

Every night Mr. Paton and his orphan children prayed for the food ship to come, and every morning the boys would rush to the beach to see if the ship was coming. But each time they returned saying sadly, "Missi, *Tavaka jimra*" (no ship yet).

Then early one morning Mr. Paton heard much shouting. *"Tavaka oa! Tavaka oa!"* (the ship, hurray), yelled the boys jumping up and down and running back and forth.

Mr. Paton and the other children ran to the beach. Joyfully they waved and waited for the ship to draw near and be unloaded. When the first barrels and boxes were brought ashore the children crowded around Mr. Paton.

"Missi, look! Here is a barrel that rattles like biscuits," they cried. "May we roll it to the house?"

What an exciting time they had rolling the big barrel up the slope! They laughed, shouted, and tumbled all over each other in their hurry.

When they had reached the house, they stood in a circle around the biscuit barrel. Eagerly they waited for Mr. Paton.

"Missi, have you forgotten what you promised us?" they asked him.

"What did I promise?"

The little dark faces looked disappointed. "Missi forgot! Missi forgot!" whispered the children to each other.

"Forgot what?" asked Mr. Paton.

"Missi, you promised that when the ship came you would give us each a biscuit."

"Oh, I didn't forget," teased the missionary. "I was only waiting to see if you remembered."

The boys and girls laughed happily. "There's no chance

23

of us forgetting. Please, will you open the barrel soon? We are dying for biscuits."

Quickly Mr. Paton grabbed a heavy hammer and bar and knocked away the end of the barrel, and handed each boy and girl a biscuit. But to his surprise not one of them began to eat. Each stood and held his biscuit in his hand.

"You are dying for biscuits," exclaimed Mr. Paton. "Why don't you eat? Are you expecting a second one?"

"No," answered one of the bigger boys, "we are just waiting to thank God for sending us food and to ask Him to bless it to us all."

In the excitement Mr. Paton had forgotten all about giving thanks. But the hungry orphan children had not. And what a glad day of thanksgiving it was for all of them!

Do you remember to give thanks for the food God sends you? Do you thank Him, too, for your parents, your homes, and all the other good things He gives you? You have so much that every day should be thanksgiving day, shouldn't it?

6

A Surprise for Mother

"Pss-st — Dale!" whispered Sally to her younger brother. "I know what we can do."

"Huh, do what?" asked Dale loudly, glancing up from his adventure-story book.

"Shh-h, Mother will hear," warned Sally, "I said, I know what we can do."

"Do about what?"

"You know," answered Sally in an impatient whisper.

Dale frowned, "I don't —." But the frown turned into a grin. "Oh, yeah, I forgot — Sunday."

"I just heard Mother tell Dad she has to go to see Mrs. Wierenga this evening. We can do it while she's gone. It won't take long. O.K.?" Dale nodded.

As soon as Mother was gone, Sally got two sheets of typing paper and pencils and crayons. She put them on the kitchen table. Then she explained, "First we'll make a card like Miss Taylor showed us in school today. We'll fold the papers in half. Like this. Then we fold them in half again. Miss Taylor says this is a French fold. It's like the cards we buy.

"Now we can draw a picture on the outside and color it. Or we can cut out a pretty picture and paste it on the cover."

Sally began to draw some dainty flowers on the cover.

Dale looked for a picture in an old magazine. At last he found a picture of a smiling woman who looked like their own mother. He cut the picture out carefully and pasted it on his card. Then he took a blue crayon and drew a border around it.

Soon Dale and Sally had finished the covers on their cards. And on each one they printed neatly, two words, TO MOTHER.

"But I don't see what's so wonderful about making our own cards for Mother on Mother's Day," said Dale looking disappointed.

"It isn't the card that's special," said Sally. "It's the gift we'll put inside." She opened her card. "On the inside we will write our gifts to Mother. We will each give her a gift of ourselves. Like, I'll write in my card, *Dear Mother, I give you my hands to make your bed every morning for two weeks. And I give my hands to wash dishes every evening without grumbling. With love, Sally.* See? And you can write a gift you will do for Mother, too. Something to help her or make her glad."

"I get it." Dale chewed his pencil thoughtfully. "But what can I give? — I know. I'll write, *Dear Mother, I give you my feet to run and get things for you. And I give my hands to make my own bed so you won't need to.*"

Carefully Dale and Sally wrote their gifts. Quickly they tucked their cards into envelopes and hid them in secret places until Sunday. They couldn't wait to see Mother's surprise and joy when she would open her Mother's Day gifts.

Have you been wishing for a special Mother's Day gift for your mother? Would you like to give her a gift of yourself, as Sally and Dale did?

7

A Happy Soul Am I

Fanny Crosby couldn't see the blue sky with cottony clouds. She couldn't see the bright flowers or the green grass. She couldn't see her frisky pet lamb. She couldn't see anything. She was blind. But Fanny didn't feel sorry for herself. When she was eight years old she wrote,

> O what a happy soul am I
> Although I cannot see,
> I am resolved that in this world
> Contented I will be.
>
> How many blessings I enjoy
> That other people don't!
> To weep and sigh because I'm blind
> I cannot and I won't.

Fanny's grandmother taught her to "see" without eyes. Her grandmother showed her how she could "see" things by touching them. Gently Fanny touched the soft petals of flowers in the garden and stooped to smell their sweet fragrance. In the woods she looked at the trees with her hands, too. She felt the rough pattern of the bark. Her fingers traced the shapes of the leaves. She learned the names of each one she saw. And she knew the birds by the songs they sang.

God's world was a beautiful place to Fanny. What fun she had wandering in the fields and woods with her grandmother and her pet lamb! And she liked to listen to the stories her grandmother told. Her favorite stories were about the Lord Jesus. Fanny believed in Him as her Saviour and wanted to please and serve Him. But what could she do?

The Lord Jesus gave this cheerful girl a joyful work to do for Him. He put thoughts in her mind and heart about Himself, and she wrote them down. Her heart was so full of love for Him that she wrote more than 8,000 poems and hymns in her lifetime. You have sung some of them in Sunday school and church. A few of the hymns she wrote are:

NEAR THE CROSS

TELL ME THE STORY OF JESUS

PASS ME NOT, O GENTLE SAVIOUR

RESCUE THE PERISHING

TO GOD BE THE GLORY

BLESSED ASSURANCE

How many of these do you know?

Dear Lord Jesus, we thank You for the songs you put in Fanny Crosby's heart. Help us to love and serve You with a happy heart too. Amen.

8

If Houses Could Talk

I stood at my open bedroom window. Sleepily I stared at the two houses across the street. And suddenly a strange thing happened. It seemed to me that the houses were talking. The white house where the Berkey family lives looked out of its windows and spoke first.

" 'Morning," it said, blinking its windows cheerfully in the bright sunlight.

"Morning yourself," answered the gray house next door, flapping its awnings lazily.

"This is my favorite day of the week," beamed the white house. "My rooms are spic and span, and I smell like the spicy cookies baked in my kitchen yesterday. I like the way my family gets up on mornings like this — not to rush to school and work but to go to church. Along with friends and neighbors they go to worship God in His house. And I have a quiet morning to myself. But I guess I like Sunday most of all because it is a happy day for my whole family. They rest, and thank and worship God in a special way."

The gray house sighed. Its awnings drooped. "Yes, I've noticed how different things are for you on Sunday. But for me it is no different from any other day. I heard my family say that Dad would scrape old paint off my east side this afternoon. Donald is going to play football. And Mother and Martha are going to sew."

The awnings of the gray house dropped still lower. "My family thinks Sunday is the time to work or do whatever each of them wants to do. It is a selfish day. Not on this

or any other day do they think of the One who gave me
and everything they have to them. They don't know or love
Him. If only they would read His Book the way I see your
family doing every day. . . . But there is nothing I can do
about it, is there?"

Sadly the gray house gazed up from under its awnings.
The white house looked thoughtfully out of its shining
windows. Both of them were silent. Then the white house
seemed to gleam as though it had a bright idea.

I waited quietly to hear what it was. But just then there

was a last call for breakfast from our kitchen. I shrugged on my robe and scampered to the breakfast table. I would have to keep moving or I would be late to church.

But I wonder what else the houses might have said that morning. And if houses did talk, what would your house say?

9

The Lost Key

Klaus, who lived in Bochum, Germany, was a *Schlüsselkind* (a key child). Like many children in German cities, he wore a key around his neck. Both his parents worked, and every day before leaving, his mother gave him the door key on a string. Klaus slipped the string over his head and tucked the key inside his shirt.

After his parents were gone, Klaus left the apartment and locked the door. Down the stairs he ran with a clatter. He dashed off to the play-park two blocks away. There he played on the swings and seesaws. Or he played *Fussball* (soccer) with some boys.

At noon Klaus hurried back to the apartment for the lunch mother had laid out. And after lunch he played again until his mother came home.

One afternoon he ran back to the apartment to get his ball. He reached inside his shirt and felt for his key. It wasn't there! It had been there at lunchtime. But now it was gone.

Where can it be? wondered Klaus. *I only took a little ride on Karl's scooter since lunch. I'll walk toward Karl's house and look on the sidewalk. It must be here somewhere.*

But it wasn't. Klaus felt like crying. But he was too big. And it wouldn't help anyway.

Then he saw Karl standing by the gate of the building where he lived. "Karl, did you see my key?" he called. "I can't find it anywhere. I must have lost it when I was riding your scooter."

"I'll help you look for it," offered Karl. "You look on one side of the walk, and I'll look on the other."

Karl looked on the left side and Klaus on the right. The key was small. It might have fallen into a crack. Or perhaps it had landed on the cobblestone street. They walked slowly, looking carefully. But they didn't find it. Sighing, they sat down on the steps in front of Klaus' home and thought.

"I know what we can do," said Karl.

"What?" asked Klaus.

"We can ask God to help us find your key. He knows where it is."

"How would He show us where it is?" asked Klaus.

"I don't know. But if He wants us to find it, we will. Of course, maybe He wants you to learn to be careful. Then He might not help. Let's ask Him and see."

Sitting on the steps, Karl and Klaus folded their hands and prayed. They asked God to help them find the lost key. Then they jumped up to look along the sidewalk another time. After a few steps Klaus shouted, "Look!" He held up the key dangling on its string. He had found it hanging on a bush.

"Oh, I remember! I had the key string in my hand. As I scooted along it must have caught on the bush."

"And God answered our prayers by helping you to see it," said Karl.

"He sure did," nodded Klaus, "Who would have looked for a key on a bush? Well, I'll run and get my ball."

"Hey, wait a minute. You forgot something."

"What?"

"To thank God for helping us."

"I . . . I didn't think of that," admitted Klaus.

So the boys sat down on the steps again and thanked God for helping them to find the lost key.

Have you asked God to help you when you needed help? How did He answer your prayers? Did you thank Him when He helped you? Does He always give you what you ask? Why not?

10

The Miracle of the Rice

The wind howled. Rain poured down. Giant waves almost swallowed the little ship. Its mast was broken, and its sails had been torn away in the terrible storm. Helplessly the ship tossed up and down and tipped from side to side. In a small room Tom Tobin and the other passengers huddled together. They wondered what was going to happen to them.

Weeks before, they had set out to go from Ireland to America in a small sailing ship. But would they ever get there? Their ship was damaged, their food was gone, and the storm kept on day after day.

Young Tom Tobin and some of the other passengers were Christians. They knew there was one thing they could do. They could pray. So they knelt together. They asked God to give them food and to bring their ship safely through the storm.

Tom and his friends did not know how God would give them food. But they believed He could. And He did. He showed them where to find food right on their ship.

Down in the ship's hold were many heavy bags. The bags helped weight the ship to make it sail better. And in those large bags was rice — a grain these people had never seen before.

Someone thought to open one of the bags to see what was in them. "Look," he called. "What is this?" Tom and the others crowded close.

"It looks like a kind of wheat," said one man.

"I have read about a grain called rice," said another, "that grows in warm, wet countries. Maybe that is what it is. I read that people use it for food."

"Let's cook some and see what happens," cried the others.

Quickly they put water into big kettles on the stove. They dumped lots of rice into the kettles. Then they waited and watched to see what would happen. The water bubbled and boiled and the rice began to cook. The grains swelled bigger and bigger, until the kettles overflowed. The men hurried to get more kettles, and the rice filled them too. The people were thrilled at this miracle of the rice.

There was more than enough fluffy, tasty rice for everyone. Happily they sat down to eat and to thank God for giving them this food. They thanked Him for causing it to be put on their ship.

The next day they put more water and rice into the kettles. Again the rice filled the pots and boiled over. The rest of their long trip they had all they could eat. And at last one day a sailor shouted the glad news that land was ahead.

What a joyful time it was when Tom and his friends landed in America over a hundred years ago! They did not forget to thank God for His goodness. They praised Him for bringing their crippled ship to shore. And they thanked Him for the miracle of the rice. All their lives they remembered how God had caused the rice to be put on their ship.

Not only at Thanksgiving but every day let us remember to thank our God for the miracle of the food He has put on earth for us to enjoy and to share.

11

Which Gift Is Best?

Are you thinking about gifts — gifts you are going to give at Christmas? Or perhaps gifts you hope to receive? Do you know what is the very best gift you can give or receive? Read this story and see.

On a little farm in China a farmer lived with three sons. The first son grew up and left the farm. He moved to a big city and became a rich businessman.

The second son grew up and left the farm, too. He took a job with the government and became an important official.

But when the third son was born, he decided to be a farmer. He bought a little farm miles away from his father's home.

The farmer missed his sons. He grew old and lonely. Because his sons were busy and far away they did not come to see him.

When the farmer was seventy-five years old, kind friends planned a birthday party for him. The three sons and many friends were invited. It was to be a happy celebration. The father was excited. Soon he would see his sons!

On his birthday the farmer sat watching and waiting for his sons to come. At last he saw a rickshaw coming up the road. "Ah, my first son," he said to himself. But when the carriage came near, he was disappointed. In it was only his son's wife.

"Isn't my son coming?" asked the old farmer.

"He is too busy, dear Father," said his daughter-in-law. "But he has a beautiful gift for you. He has bought you a little home in the village. It will be much nicer than this farmhouse."

The old man smiled sadly, "That is a fine gift," he said.

Just then he saw another carriage coming up the road. *There, that must be my second son,* he thought. But in the rickshaw was only his second daughter-in-law.

"Your second son is sorry he could not come," she said. "He is sending you a gift you will enjoy using. It is a pretty carriage and he is sending a man to pull it for you."

"That is kind of him," nodded the old man slowly. But he looked sad. He kept watching the road and waiting for his youngest son. Finally, he saw a group of people walking up the road. It was the third son, and behind him came his family. The old father beamed. He hurried to meet his son and to greet his wife and family.

The third son bowed his head politely. "Father, I am sorry we are late," he said, "and I am sorry we could not bring you a gift. My farm is small and the crops were poor

37

this year. All we could do is come to see you and tell you we love you."

The old farmer wiped away happy tears and said, "My son, you have brought me the best gift of all. You came yourself to tell me you loved me!"

Christmas is the birthday of our Saviour who was born on earth to make a way for us to live in heaven. What will you give Him on His birthday? Most of all He wants you to trust Him as your Saviour and to give Him your love. Will He be disappointed?

—Adapted

12

Books

If I could come to visit you I would surely find books in your home. And you might want to show me your favorite ones. Perhaps you would tell me about them. But can you imagine how strange it would be to live in a world without books?

Every year thousands and thousands of new books are printed. There are all kinds and sizes of them. There are history books, story books, picture books, birthday books, autograph books, puzzle and paint books and even bank books. And there are good books and bad ones.

Are you careful what books you read? Do you know that what you read will be written in your mind? I am sure you want to "write" only good things there.

The most important book in your home is the one that tells you the Way to God and heaven — the Bible. It is really many books in one. It has history, adventure, poetry, songs, and pictures painted in words. In it are stories about kings, shepherds, wars and warriors, fishermen, and brave children. Best of all it is the story of the Lord Jesus who loves you and who gave His life for you — for your sins.

But did you know that there are books in heaven? There is the *Book of Life,* in which appear the names of all who trust in Jesus as their Savior. And when God shall judge people, He will open this Book. Those whose names are in it He will welcome to heaven. They will live with Him forever. Is your name in His *Book of Life?*

Another book He has is the *Book of Remembrance.*

What do you think is recorded in such a book? It is a record of the deeds of boys and girls and men and women who belong to the Savior. He will reward all who are true and faithful to Him. Do you think this book will have a record of some things you have done for Him?

One day the Lord Jesus is coming again to take those who belong to Him to be with Him. And when He comes He will have His rewards with Him. He said,

"Behold I come quickly and my reward is
with me, to give everyone according as
his deeds" (Revelation 22:12).

Prayer: Dear Father in heaven, I thank You for the many good books we have to read. And I thank You for the best book, the Bible. I thank You, too, for the Books of Life and of Remembrance. Write my name in Your Book of Life for I love and trust in the Lord Jesus. Amen.

13

The Strange Zoo

Where am I? How did I get here? wondered Bill. He looked about in surprise. He seemed to be alone in the middle of a zoo. All around him were cages. He strolled up to the nearest one. A huge grumpy-looking bear stared out at him. Bill glanced at the sign on the cage. How strange! It did not tell anything about the bear. There was only one word on the sign — Grumbling. *Well, you look grouchy all right,* thought Bill as he turned away.

He moved along to the next cage. In it stood a homely mule shaking his head slowly from side to side. Bill laughed. He could not help it. The mule looked foolish and silly. On the sign on his cage was the word Stubbornness. "Stubbornness," muttered Bill to himself. "That could be your name. It suits the way you look and act."

Just then a terrible *r-rr-roar* filled the air. Bill jumped and looked for a place to hide. But there was none. From a distance he peered cautiously into the gloomy cage from which the loud roar had come. A big lion was pacing back and forth in it. He switched his tail jerkily and glared fiercely at Bill. "I'm sure glad you are locked up," said Bill. "You look mean and cross. I wonder what your sign says. Ho — Anger. Yep, you look exactly like I feel sometimes when I'm mad."

Slowly Bill walked on to the other cages. In one he saw a sly weasel named Thief. In another slithered a snake

named Deceit. And there was Pride, a strutting peacock; Envy, a snarling tiger; and Greed, a fat pig. Bill stopped and scratched his head. "This is the strangest zoo I ever saw."

Then he heard a voice. It sounded like Dad's. He looked around but he could not see anyone anywhere. The voice said, "Bill, you have been looking at the zoo of the heart."

"The zoo of the heart?" repeated Bill, puzzled.

"Yes," answered the voice. "For 'from men's hearts come evil thoughts, stealing, murder, greed, wickedness, deceit, envy, gossip, pride, and foolishness!' These wild things must not be allowed loose in your heart. They must be locked up and put away."

Bill nodded his head.

The voice continued, "Only one Person can lock them up and put them away for you. And then, instead of them He will fill your heart with kindness, cheerfulness, love, obedience, humility, and good things."

"I know who the Person is," said Bill, "And. . . ." But he got no further. All of a sudden we woke up and discovered that he was not in the zoo. He was lying in his bed. He had been dreaming. Slowly he sat up. He pulled his knees up and propped his elbows on them. He thought, *Anyway it is not just a dream that there are wild things in my heart. There are. And it is real that I need the only Person who can lock them up and put them away.*

Prayer: Dear Lord Jesus, be the keeper of my heart. Cleanse it from evil and help me to do that which pleases You. Amen.

14

The High-flying Chicken

About twenty years ago a strange thing happened in far-away north China.

A little baby had just been born to a missionary family. Quickly the nurse wrapped the new baby in a warm blanket. Then she got down on her knees and laid it *under* the bed. You see, there was an air raid going on. There was war in China. Now and then enemy planes zoomed over the city and dropped big bombs. Wherever the bombs fell they exploded with a terrible boom and blew buildings to bits.

The enemies must not have known that the people had left the city. It was empty — empty except for three missionary families and their faithful Chinese helpers. During the air raid the missionaries stayed inside. There was nothing they could do to protect themselves. So they trusted God to care for them. And He did. Soon the planes roared away and it was quiet again.

The nurse got the little baby from under the bed. As she tucked it into its own crib she thought, *I wish I had some tasty food for the baby's mother. She is weak and tired. But the cupboard is almost as bare as old Mother Hubbard's. There is only flour left in it.*

There were no eggs or vegetables. There was no fruit or meat and no place to buy these things nor anyone to buy from.

If I only had some meat, wished the nurse to herself. And then it happened. Right over the twenty-foot wall flew a chicken! With a thump it landed on the ground near the house. The surprised nurse and the missionaries could not believe their eyes. A real live chicken!

They hurried to look outside the gate and all around. Where could it have come from? Each family had taken their chickens and food with them when they fled.

So the chicken became nourishing broth and meat for the mother of the new baby. How the delighted nurse and missionaries thanked God for the high-flying chicken which had come across the wall!

I think the missionaries may have thought of God's promise in I Peter 5:7 which says, "He cares for you." And perhaps they sang a song like,

> Be not dismayed what-e'er betide,
>   God will take care of you;
> Beneath His wings of love abide,
>   God will take care of you.
> All you may need He will provide,
>   God will take care of you;
> Nothing you ask will be denied,
>   God will take care of you.

—Adapted

15

A Surprise for the President

There was a tap on the door of the President's office. The door opened. The President looked up from his work. A little, gray-haired lady carrying a basket was ushered into the room. The President unfolded himself and stood up politely. He invited the lady to be seated.

"What can I do for you, Madam?" he asked kindly.

The lady put her small basket on the President's desk. She smiled, "Oh, I have not come to ask a favor. I heard that you are very fond of cookies. I only came to bring you this basket of cookies."

The tired President straightened his shoulders in surprise. For a moment he did not say a word. Tears glistened
in his eyes. He blinked. Then he said in a deep voice.
"My good woman, your thoughtful and unselfish deed
greatly moves me. Thousands have come into this office
since I became president, and you are the first one to come
asking no favor for yourself or for someone else."

The surprised President was none other than Abraham
Lincoln.

Can you think of Someone to whom people today often
go only to ask for things? Yes, many boys and girls and
men and women pray to God only to ask Him for things.
They do not think of showing Him love.

16

The Color of Days

Mother opened Gary's bedroom door.

"Ga-a-ry — breakfast," she called cheerfully.

Slowly Gary stretched his legs and then his arms. He
yawned and opened his eyes sleepily. "What color is today?"
he mumbled.

"Color?" repeated Mother raising one eyebrow. "Are
you sure you are awake?"

"Yup," grinned Gary. He pulled up his legs and sprang out of bed to prove it.

Mother shook her head and returned to the kitchen.

At breakfast a few minutes later Gary explained about the color of days.

"Days do have colors, Mom. Why, when it rains in the spring or summer the days are green — wet green.

Mother nodded and took a sip of coffee.

"But if the sun shines very bright and the sky is very blue and the clouds look like cotton, it is a blue and white day."

Gary bit off a big piece of cinnamon toast and almost swallowed it whole. "If a day is cloudy and very foggy then it has a soft gray color."

"Mm-mm," agreed Mother and dropped another slice of bread into the toaster.

"In autumn when the leaves are yellow, red and brown and the sun shines, the days have a golden color. But snowy winter days are white and black." Gary stopped to eat more toast.

"Nights have colors, too. Some are black. You know,

48

nights when clouds cover up the stars. Clear nights are blue-black and speckled. And moonlight nights are silvery."

Mother poured herself another cup of coffee. "I guess I never thought much about the color of our days and nights. But I'm glad you have. I guess you noticed because you like to paint pictures. I think it pleases the Lord when we notice the lovely things he made for us to enjoy. You reminded me of a Bible verse we should say to ourselves at the beginning of each new day whatever its color may be.

"This is the day which the Lord has made;
let us be glad and rejoice in it."

Mother pushed back the white curtains and looked out of the window. "I think this is going to be a bright blue and white day. Let's thank the Lord for it and ask Him to help us use its minutes and hours in ways that please Him."

Prayer: Lord Jesus, we thank You for this new day. Guide us in all we do and say. Help us all day to do what pleases You. We know this is the only way to be happy and to make others happy, too. Amen.

49

17

A Letter That Couldn't Be Mailed

Jim sat at his desk and stared at the zig-zag crack in the wall. But he didn't really see the crack. He was thinking. His teacher, Mr. Weaver, had said, "Today, let's write a letter of thanks to someone. We will each write to a friend or a relative to thank them for something they have given us or done for us. I'll give each one of you a sheet of writing paper and an envelope to put it in. Then you can mail the letter if you like."

Jim was trying to decide to whom he would write his letter of thanks. Suddenly he sat up straight. He had an idea. He smiled to himself at his good idea. *I know what I'll do,* he thought. *I'll write to the Person who loves me most of all and has done the most for me.*

He picked up his pencil and began to write. He wrote carefully in big, round letters. He tried to stay on the lines. It didn't take him long. He knew just what he wanted to say. Soon he was finished. He signed his name plainly below his letter and folded it to fit into the envelope.

At last all the other children were finished writing their

letters. Then Mr. Weaver said, "Before you put your letters into the envelope you may read them to the class."

One after the other the boys and girls stood and read their letters. There were letters to uncles, grandmothers, dads, mothers, cousins, brothers, and sisters. There were long letters, short letters, funny letters, and happy letters. Finally, it was Jim's turn to read what he had written. He stood and read.

Dear God,

I'm writing this letter to thank you for the best gift in the world. I thank you for giving Jesus to be my Saviour. I know you love me very much. You gave Jesus to die on the cross for me. Thank you for forgiving my sins because I believe in Him.

Please be with me. Keep me from doing wrong.

With love,

—Jim

It was very quiet in the room when Jim sat down. The children looked at each other in surprise. Not one of them had ever thought of writing a letter to God.

Mr. Weaver was pleased with all the letters but especially with Jim's. He said, "We were remembering to thank others for their gifts and kindness to us. But Jim's letter reminds us not to forget to say 'thank you' to God, too. The Bible says, 'It is a good thing to give thanks unto the Lord' (Psalm 92:1)."

Why did Jim decide to write his letter to God? Do you believe God loves you and sent Jesus to die for your sins, too? Did you ever tell Him? How can you tell Him and thank Him?

18

Freddie's Neighbor

It was Friday afternoon. Little Freddie was going to visit his friend Billy, who lived around the corner. Just then three big boys who were teasing and tussling came down the street. One of them bumped into Freddie and knocked him down. Little Freddie skinned his knee on the rough pavement. And he bumped his head against a tree. It frightened him and he began to cry.

At that moment nine-year-old Bruce, who lived in the same block raced by on his bicycle. He saw Freddie crying, but he did not think of stopping. He was on his way to church for his Cub Scout meeting. A visitor from the city baseball team was going to give them some tips about baseball. Bruce did not want to be late.

Right after Bruce whizzed by, Mark, who went to Freddie's Sunday school, came along. Mark never missed Sunday school, and he knew many Bible verses by heart. He even knew some about being kind. But he did not stop to help little Freddie either. He barely bothered to look at him. Mark was on his way to the store. Little Freddie cried and cried.

But then dark eyed, dark-skinned Manuel came along. He was a new boy who had moved into one of the houses near the corner. Most of the children did not talk to him or play with him. He was a stranger and they did not like him. He was different. But when Manuel saw Freddie crying, he stopped. "What's wrong little boy?" he asked.

He helped Freddie stand up and with his handkerchief he wiped away the little boy's tears.

"Come," he said, "We will go to my house. My mother will bandage your knee. Then you can tell me where you live. I'll walk home with you. Everything will be all right."

Freddie's head and knee still hurt, but he stopped crying. Soon Manuel's mother had washed his bleeding knee and put a soft bandage on it. She held a cool damp cloth on his head and she gave him a sugar cookie. Afterward Manuel took Freddie home to his mother.

Can you tell

1. Of what Bible story, told by Jesus, does this remind you? If you can't think of it, read Luke 10:30-37.

2. Who was Manuel like?

3. What about Bruce and Mark?

Bible Words: "Do not let our love be just words. . . . let it be true and show itself in acts" (I John 3:18).

53

19

The Best Tools

Whenever Tommy was missing, everyone knew where to find him — in Uncle Don's workshop. It was his favorite place. Uncle Don's workshop was fascinating! It was crammed full of interesting pieces of wood and iron, and jars of bolts, nails, and screws. Best of all, hanging on the walls were tools of many shapes and sizes. And Tommy loved tools. Often he would point to one and ask, "Uncle Don, what's that? What's it for?"

Jolly Uncle Don liked boys who asked questions. Gladly would he take down the tool and tell curious Tommy its name and how it was used. Soon Tommy knew the names of most of the chisels, scrapers, saws, hammers, punches, and other tools. What fun he had learning how to use some of them with Uncle Don's help!

"When I grow up I'm going to have a workshop and make things like you do," Tommy confided to Uncle Don. "But tools cost a lot of money, don't they?"

"Yes, good tools are expensive," agreed his uncle, nodding. "Of course, when I started my shop I had only a few. Whenever I had enough money I bought others until I finally had all I needed. . . . But, Tommy, you already have one set of tools you need — the most wonderful tools of all."

I have a set of wonderful tools? Tommy was puzzled. *I don't know what Uncle Don is talking about. He must be teasing.* "Well, I don't have any real tools yet," he said, "just play ones."

"Oh, yes you do." Uncle Don reached down, lifted up Tommy's hands, and placed them on the workbench. "There they are," he smiled. "Look at what fine tools you have. They have strong bones and muscles to give them power, blood to keep them warm, a special system to lubricate them, nerves to flash messages from your mind so they know what to do. And over the bone, muscles, and nerves is a stretch-glove of skin." Uncle Don touched Tommy's pink-skinned hand.

"See, this glove of skin does not wear off even though you wear it all the time. If it gets a cut or a hole it repairs itself. Your hands keep themselves repaired and ready for

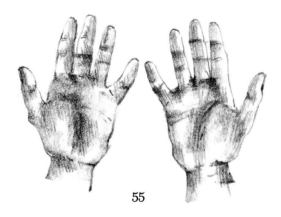

your use. Yet you hardly notice them or think about them, do you?"

Tommy looked at his hands as though he had not really seen them before.

"Hands are such wonderful tools that they can do thousands of different jobs," continued Uncle Don. "They are used by doctors, nurses, mechanics, farmers, watch-makers, teachers, artists, musicians, builders, typists, and by all other kinds of workers. Only our great wise God could have planned and made tools as fine and useful as these."

20

The Do-what-you-want Day

"Ah, Mom," begged Ned. "I don't feel like practicing. Do I have to?"

"Yes," answered Mother firmly, "Tomorrow is your lesson day."

Ned flopped down onto the piano bench. Slowly he thumped a melody with one finger. Then he flipped a page and played another tune the same way. Plunk, plunk, plunkity plunk, plunk.

Finally Mother said, "All right Ned, that's enough. You may go play until dinner is ready." And away Ned dashed for a ball game with his friends.

After dinner that evening Mother said, "Ned, please take a book over to Mrs. Dean for me."

"Ah, Mom," began Ned, and Mother knew just what he was going to say — what he always said when she asked him to do something. "I don't feel like it. Do I have to?"

Mother smiled and nodded her head. Grumpily Ned trudged down the street to Mrs. Dean's house.

The next morning after breakfast, Mother asked, "Ned, will you please empty the waste basket for me?"

Without thinking he answered, "I don't feel like it. Do I have to?"

He waited for Mother to say, "Yes." But she didn't. She said, "No, you don't have to. I've decided that you and I will have a do-what-you-want day. We'll just do what we want to do."

"You mean I don't have to practice or take my piano lesson, or study, or even go to school?" asked Ned. He couldn't believe his ears!

"Yes, we will both do only what we feel like doing."

"Oh boy," grinned Ned, "That's a swell idea."

Off he went to watch the men and machines at work on a

57

new street. Then he rode his bike around the neighborhood for a while. How quiet and lonely it seemed! Next he played with his trucks and cars. Somehow it wasn't much fun to play alone.

Lunch time came. But Mother must have forgotten. She was reading a book. "How about lunch, Mom?" asked Ned.

"Oh, I don't feel like getting lunch," said Mother. "You just eat whatever you like."

So he munched some peanut-butter and crackers, and wandered out to play. In a short time he came back into the house for a drink of milk and more crackers. He wished Mother had made him a real lunch.

Then he remembered there was a button off his baseball suit. He showed it to his mother. "Look, Mom, would you sew a button on my suit?"

"I'm busy knitting now," answered Mother. "I don't want to sew. Why don't you do it yourself?"

Me sew on a button? Ned shook his head. He hung the suit on a doorknob and went to get his bat and ball. Let's see, where had he put them last evening? He looked and looked. "Mom," he called. "I can't find my bat and ball. Will you help me look for them?"

But Mother didn't feel like helping him. And when supper time came she was still knitting. No hot supper waited for a hungry boy. He could help himself, Mother said, and eat whatever he wanted to.

Ned frowned. A do-what-you-want day didn't seem like such a great idea after all. "You know, Mom" he announced. "I like it better when we do things for each other instead of just whatever we feel like doing."

"So do I," agreed Mother smiling.

21

Safe Harbor

What fun it is to visit a breezy, busy harbor! There you can watch big ships glide through deep, dark water. Or see little tugboats chugging back and forth about their work. Or you can wave at friendly sailors.

Becky and Mark love to visit the harbor near their home. On warm summer days they go to their grandfather and beg, "Grandpa, please take us to watch ships today."

Grandfather used to be a captain on a freighter, and if he is not busy he gladly goes to the harbor with Becky and Mark. Then he tells them stories about ships, harbors and sailors.

Already Becky and Mark know a lot about different kinds of ships. And they are learning to read the harbor traffic signs. Have you ever noticed the traffic signs in a harbor? Do you know what they mean?

The ocean, and the channel from it into the harbors, are charted and marked by buoys. Buoys are the traffic signs placed in the water to guide ships' pilots.

If you were on a ship entering a harbor you would see that the channel was marked on your right side by red buoys and on the left by black ones. And you could tell where the middle of the channel was because it is marked by buoys with black and white up-and-down stripes.

But a buoy with black and white bands around it shows where the fishermen have put out their nets and traps. And black and red up-and-down-stripes on a buoy means there is an obstruction — something sticking up under the water.

Or it marks the place where two channels meet. A white-colored buoy marks the anchorages — the places where ships may anchor.

There are many kinds of buoys in harbors and in the ocean. Some have white, green, or red lights and some have lights that flash off and on. Still others whistle or ring a bell. Each buoy marker is there to help guide ships to reach harbors safely.

Becky and Mark's grandfather says that all of us are like ships on the ocean of life and that there are special buoys to mark our way on this ocean, too. Do you know where these buoys can be seen? What do you think they tell us? The buoys for our lives are found in the Bible. In it God plainly tells us about the dangers on the ocean of life. And He shows us the only safe channel for our lives. But best of all, if we trust in Him and in His Son, He Himself will pilot us safely across the ocean of life into the safe harbor of His home.

22

How the Dumfries Was Saved

The Captain of the *Dumfries*, a double-masted sailing-ship, was worried. There was no wind to fill the sails of his ship. A strong water-current was carrying it the wrong direction. The current was taking the ship dangerously close to some sand reefs. The Captain and his sailors did everything they could to turn the ship away from the reefs. But nothing they did worked. The ship drifted nearer and nearer to the reefs.

The Captain stood on deck and watched helplessly. Then he turned to the only passenger, James Hudson Tay-

lor, and said, "Well, we have done everything that we can. We can only wait for what is going to happen."

Suddenly Mr. Taylor had an idea.

"No, there is one thing we have not yet done."

"What is that?" asked the surprised Captain.

"Well, four of us on board are Christians. Let each of us go to his own cabin and ask God to send a breeze immediately."

The Captain, who was one of the Christians, agreed. The four men hurried to their cabins, knelt down, and prayed. After Mr. Taylor had prayed, he was sure God would send the breeze they needed. He went to the deck officer and said, "Will you let down the corners of the mainsail?"

"What would be the use of that?" asked the man roughly.

"We have asked God to send a wind. And it is coming right away."

The man cursed. "I'd rather see it than hear tell about it," he said. But as he spoke the corner of the topmost sail began to flutter gently.

"Don't you *see* the wind is coming? Look!" cried Mr. Taylor.

"No, it is only a cat's paw (a little puff of breeze)," grumbled the officer.

"Put down the mainsail!" urged Mr. Taylor. There was not a minute to lose. The ship was almost on the reef.

Then the man let it down quickly, for the wind had really begun to blow. And it was just in time to save the *Dumfries*.

The Captain heard all the noise on deck and came running to find out what was happening. How thankful he was to see how God had answered their prayers! He was thankful, too, for Mr. Taylor, who had reminded him to pray.

The passenger with the idea was a missionary on his way to China more than 100 years ago. At that time he was only twenty-one years old. But he lived to see God answer many other prayers and to become a famous missionary.

23

Signposts

It was the day after Halloween. Dad, Mother, Mark, and Sue Marshall were taking a trip. Their favorite uncle and aunt had moved to their state. So they were going to Littleton to visit them. After driving all morning they were beginning to get tired.

Suddenly they saw a crossroad with a sign which read, 5 miles to Littleton. Mark bounced up and down on the

seat. "Yippee!" he shouted. "We're almost there."

They turned in the direction the sign pointed — north. The road wasn't very good. It took them through a woods, over some hills and across a bumpy railroad track. They drove and drove. But there was no town. It seemed as if they had driven much more than five miles. Finally, Dad decided to stop at a farmhouse to ask directions.

"Oh," said the farmer, "you are going in the wrong direction. You must turn around. Littleton is thirteen miles south of here."

Dad told the farmer about the signpost that pointed north. The farmer looked surprised and scratched his head. Then he smiled. "You know, Mister, last night was Halloween. I reckon some boys playing tricks must have turned that sign around."

So the Marshalls turned their car around and went back to take the right road. But no one changed the sign. And for days many people traveling along that road turned the wrong way.

You know, if we are Christians we are like signposts. Many people look to us for direction. If we live for Jesus our lives point the right way for others to go. But if we don't live for Him, we point the wrong way. Then people will be led astray. Which way does the signpost of your life point others to go?

24

Paper That Spoke

(Based on a true story)

"Boana," called the missionary.

"Yes, sir," answered the dark boy as he popped his head around a corner.

The missionary smiled at his helper. "Please take this paper to the man at the plantation store," he said.

Boana took the piece of paper the missionary gave him.

He held it tight in his hand and skipped down the path toward the store. All along the way were exciting things to see. On the ground he saw tracks made by two pigs. Ahead of him a startled snake slithered into the grass. Several busy rats scurried across the path. Bright butterflies fluttered around him. Big beautiful birds flew back and forth between the trees. Feathery ferns waved in the breeze. And red and yellow flowers nodded at him.

Before he knew it Boana was at the plantation store. He walked up to the store man and gave him the missionary's paper. He waited to see what the man would do with it. First the man stood still and looked at the paper. Then he got a box and put some little packages and tin cans in it. He looked at the paper again and put another package in the box. Then the man picked up the box and gave it to the surprised Boana to carry to the missionary.

I don't understand, thought Boana. *That must have been a magic paper. It spoke to the store man. It told him to give me these things for the missionary. It is big magic. I must tell my father about it. Maybe we can get some magic paper, too.*

Boana hurried. He stopped only twice to rest even though the box was heavy. He couldn't wait to tell his family about the paper that could talk.

How surprised the missionary was to see Boana back so quickly! The missionary praised him and gave him three blue buttons to put on the string around his neck. Boana thanked the missionary shyly. Then he slipped out of the house and ran home as fast as his brown legs would go.

"Father, Mother, Brother, Sister," he called, "The missionary has magic paper!" And he told them what had happened when he took the missionary's paper to the store.

Boana's father looked thoughtful. "The missionary is a kind man," he said, "We will ask him for some of his magic paper. But first we must tell the other men in the village."

Boana had to tell about the magic paper again and again until all the men had heard about it. Then the men had a meeting. They said, "We will go and ask the missionary for some of the paper that can speak."

In the evening they all marched to the missionary's home. They stood politely outside his house and coughed and made little noises so he would know he had visitors.

"Mr. Missionary," said Boana's father, "My son has told us about your magic paper. He told us that he took a piece of it to the store and it spoke to the store man. The store man gave him things for you. And we have come to ask you to give us some of this magic paper, too."

The missionary invited the men to sit down on the grass with him. Then he explained the secret of the paper. He said, "I made marks on the paper I gave to Boana. The marks were words. The words told the store man what I wanted. But I pay him for all the things I ordered."

The men couldn't understand. It still seemed like magic to them because none of them could read or write. They had no paper and no books.

The missionary saw how puzzled the men were and he had an idea. "I tell you what I'll do," he said, "If you will send your children to my home, I'll teach them to make marks on paper. They can learn to make paper speak and to know what it says."

So a school was started in that part of the island of New Guinea. Boana and other happy boys began to learn the secrets of paper that speaks. It was not easy, but they thought it was fun. Secretly they still hoped it would make them rich.

Soon they discovered that paper was not magic. It did not bring them clothes, food, and other things. But it brought them something much, much better, for they learned to hear a very special Book speak. The Book spoke to their hearts. It told them how to be rich in their hearts.

It told them of the Great God who made their island and the blue ocean around it.

It told them that God loved men, women, boys and girls.

It told them that God gave His Son to be punished for the wrong things they did.

It told them that He would forgive the wrong things they had done if they would trust in Him.

And it told them of a lovely place He is getting ready for those who trust in Him.

Boana and some of the children and parents believed what the Book said and were made rich and glad in their hearts.

25

Open Line

More than a hundred years ago Cyrus Field had an exciting idea. He dreamed of putting a telegraph cable across the Atlantic ocean between America and England. A cable would make it possible to send messages back and forth quickly. But to make the cable would be very expensive. And to lay it across so many miles of ocean would be difficult.

Mr. Field presented his idea to the British and American governments. They were interested and gave large sums of money toward the project.

A cable was made and the hard work of laying it began. But after 360 miles of the cable were laid it snapped, and the men had to start over again. A year later they tried another time. After long, careful work they managed to get the cable laid the whole way. There was great excitement when messages began to be sent back and forth. But that cable also broke.

It didn't seem that Mr. Field could try again. His money was gone. His business had failed, and his office had burned. Everything had gone wrong. Yet he did not give up.

It took him seven years to raise enough money for the next try. This time the cable broke 1,200 miles out. Still the determined man would not quit. A fourth cable was made and laid. It had cost years of work and great amounts of money. But at last Mr. Field succeeded. Telegraph communication between America and Europe was possible.

You know, a way of communication between heaven and earth has been planned and made. Jesus made a way for sinners like us to talk with God who is holy. The cost to Him was great. He had to leave heaven and come to earth to die on the cross for our sin. But he did not have to try and fail and try again to find the right way. He knew exactly what to do, and He did it. By His death He opened a new and living way to God — a new way of communication between heaven and earth. And all those who trust in Him may speak to God in heaven anytime.

Prayer: Dear heavenly Father, we thank You for Jesus. We thank You that He has made a way for us to talk with You anytime, anywhere. Amen.

26

The Missionary Garden

Tom's back ached. His hands were getting red and sore. But he didn't stop. Back and forth, back and forth his garden rake went. How fine it made the soil!

Tom and Cindy were making a little garden next to Father's big one. It was hard work. Cindy's finger nails were filled with dirt and her hands were brown with it. But she didn't mind. With her hoe she made a straight row where Tom had raked and raked. Then she bent down and carefully dropped carrot seeds into it.

When Tom was finished raking he helped Cindy sow red beet and lettuce seeds. Using his rake he covered them lightly with earth. Then together he and Cindy stuck two

rows of tiny onions into the ground. And last of all, Father helped them plant three rows of potatoes.

"Hey, what are you doing?" asked Dave, the neighbor boy, looking over the fence.

"We're planting a missionary garden," said Tom.

"A what?" frowned Dave.

"A missionary garden," answered Tom.

"What kind of a garden is that?" Dave wanted to know.

"Well," explained Tom, "Cindy and I want to give some money to Uncle Don and Aunt Gertrude — they're missionaries in Korea. We thought and thought about what we could do to earn some money. So we decided to make a garden and grow onions, carrots, and things. We can sell them and send the money to Uncle Don and Aunt Gertrude."

"Yes," said Cindy proudly, "Uncle Don and Aunt Gertrude tell the Korean boys and girls about the Lord Jesus. They buy Bibles for daddies, mothers and children who don't have any. And they buy food and clothes for some boys and girls who live in an orphanage."

"Could I work in your missionary garden and help you to sell what you grow?" Dave wondered.

"Sure," agreed Tom. "My back tells me we could use help. We can take turns raking and hoeing our garden. We'll have the best one in town."

So Tom, Dave, and Cindy had a missionary garden to help Korean children know about the Saviour who loves them and who died for their sins.

What can you do to help other boys and girls know about the Lord Jesus?

27

Two Mice and a Pony

One day Tim and Don's grandfather brought two little glass and wire cages to their house. In each cage was a tiny white mouse. Grandfather gave the cages to the boys. He said, "I'd like you to take care of these mice for me. I'll show you what to feed them and how to clean their cages.

Tim listened carefully to grandfather. He did just what grandfather said. Everyday he fed the little mouse and kept his cage clean. The little mouse twinkled his whiskers happily. He was contented and comfortable.

But Don thought it was too much bother to care for a mouse. He was lazy. Many times he forgot to feed him. And he didn't keep his cage clean. In a short time the poor mouse was not healthy or happy.

Weeks later grandfather came to see how his mice were getting along. He was pleased to see the mouse he had given Tim. He praised Tim for doing a good job. But when he saw the one he had given Don he looked sad.

"You didn't do what I asked," he said. "You didn't think it was important to look after a tiny mouse. So I'll give him to Tim."

"And since Tim cared so well for the mouse I gave him I think he is just the boy I can trust to care for the pony I want to give away."

Don hung his head. How sorry he was that he had been lazy and careless!

Why did grandfather give Tim the pony?

Is it important for you to learn to be faithful in little jobs?

Why?

If the Lord Jesus is your Saviour and Master do you think it matters how you serve Him?

Prayer: Dear Lord Jesus help me to love and obey You. Help me to be faithful in each little thing You give me to do. Amen.

To those who obey Him Jesus says,

"Well done you good and faithful-servant; you have been faithful over little, I will put you in charge of much."

Matthew 25:23

28

An Offering for the River God

Have you ever seen a crocodile at the zoo? Was he lying perfectly still in brownish water? You probably had to look twice to see him. Perhaps all you could see was his nostrils, the bumps of his eyes, and part of his back sticking out of the water. He may have looked like a harmless floating log. But he is not harmless — he is dangerous.

Do you know what would happen if an animal should wander too close to the crocodile? Quick as a flash the crocodile's strong jaws would snap hold of a leg and he would drag the careless animal under water.

Years ago some people in India thought the crocodile was sacred. They worshiped him as one of their gods. Before laws were made against it, mothers used to offer their children to the crocodiles in the river. Why did they do that? They thought it would please this river god.

One day two missionaries walked along a certain river path. At the river's edge sat an Indian mother staring at the dark water. In her arms the mother cradled a sickly baby girl. And nearby her healthy dark-skinned son laughed and played happily.

The missionaries looked sad. They guessed what the Indian mother meant to do. She was planning to give one of her children to the crocodiles. The missionaries stopped and sat down to talk with her. They told her the story of Jesus.

"Don't give your dear children to the river god," begged the missionaries. "Trust in Jesus. He is the only Savior."

"All my life I have worshiped the river god," said the mother. "What you tell me is so new and strange. I just can't believe it."

At last the missionaries walked away sadly.

A few days later they met the Indian mother again. This time only one child was with her — the sick baby girl. The missionaries sighed. They knew what must have happened. The mother's healthy son had been given to the crocodiles.

"If you thought you had to give one of your children, why didn't you give the poor, sick baby?" asked the missionaries.

The mother's dark eyes flashed. She stood straight and tall. "We give our best to our gods," she answered proudly.

I wonder — do we give our best to the true God of heaven and earth? What is our best? It is to give Him ourselves while we are young so our whole lives may be lived for Him. Have you given Him your best?

29

The Foolish Pilot

What a busy, interesting place an airport is! Some planes landing and loading, others refueling or roaring off into the sky!

Do you suppose planes just come and go as they please at an airport? No, there are traffic rules for them to follow. There are rules for them to follow in the air and on the ground. The pilot of each plane is told when and where he may land. And he is told when and where he may take off.

Have you ever noticed a high-windowed tower at the airport? That is the control tower. In it sit the men who direct the plane traffic at the airfield. They tell the pilots which runway to use and when it is clear to land or take off.

One day at a certain airport a planeload of people was all ready to take off. Down the runway the big plane roared — faster and faster. But suddenly before it left the ground the pilot braked. He braked the plane as hard as he could. The passengers were jerked forward in their seats. The plane swerved and came to a frightening stop. The startled passengers all began talking at once. "What's wrong? What happened? Why did we stop?" they asked.

Why did the pilot stop the plane so suddenly? A small plane was crossing the runway the big plane was using. The foolish pilot of the small plane had not asked or listened for directions from the control tower. He just started off. Did he think he did not need instructions? How careless and how foolish! He almost lost his own life and his plane. And many people could have been killed.

Do you think we might be in danger of being as foolish as that pilot? You know, if we should try to live our lives our own way we would be even more foolish than he. For all of us need guidance. We need someone who sees and knows what is ahead of us on life's runways. We need a wise guide — a guide who can tell us what is best to do and when to do it. And the Lord Jesus is just such a guide. The Bible says, "In all your ways acknowledge him, and he shall direct your paths" (Proverbs 3:6).

30

Philip's Escape

It was a sticky day in central Africa. The air was hot and still; not a leaf stirred. Near a certain mission home a little boy named Philip was playing. He was playing in the shade of a big tree. Suddenly he heard his father call sharply. "Philip, do exactly what I say — get down on your stomach."

Philip obeyed at once. He dropped to the ground.

"Crawl fast toward me," ordered his father.

The boy crawled as fast as his arms and legs would go. When he was half way to where his father stood, his father said, "All right, you may stand up now and run the rest of the way." Quickly Philip scrambled to his feet and ran to his father.

"Turn and look back at the tree," said the father. Philip turned and looked. His eyes opened wide. Guess what he saw! There hanging down from the branch under which he had been playing was a big snake. A snake fifteen feet long!

Philip's quick obedience very likely saved his life. By obeying his father at once he escaped the dangerous snake.

Would you have been as prompt to obey as Philip was? Do you obey your parents, your teachers, your baby sitter, or the school traffic captains promptly? And most important of all, do you obey Jesus? Have you heard Him say,

"Come to me?" If you come to Jesus He will save you from an enemy more dangerous than a snake. He will save you from Satan who is called *that old Serpent.*

> Little children, come to Jesus;
> Hear Him saying, "Come to me";
> Blessed Jesus, who to save us
> Shed His blood on Calvary.
> Little souls were made to serve Him,
> All His holy law fulfill;
> Little hearts were made to love Him,
> Little hands to do His will.
> —Adapted from *Eternity* magazine with permission

31

The Slug

Paul and Dick strolled up to the bubble-gum machine in Mr. Swanson's store.

"Wish we had a nickel," sighed Paul, staring at the rainbow-colored balls.

"How about the one you found yesterday?" asked Dick.

"It's not a real nickel," explained Paul. He reached into

his pocket, got out the coin, and held it up. "See, it's only a piece of metal that looks like a nickel. It's a slug."

"Hey, why don't we put it into the machine and see what happens?" suggested Dick. "If it works we'll get some gum. Mr. Swanson won't know who put it in."

Paul looked at the slug again. *That wouldn't be honest. It would be stealing,* said a voice inside him.

But quickly he stuck the piece of metal into the slot and turned the crank. Five balls of gum fell into his hand. The boys grinned at each other in surprise. Paul rolled a red ball into Dick's hand. He popped a green one into his mouth. The others he dropped into his pocket. Their cheeks bulging, the boys left the store. Slowly they walked up the street to Bud's house to play.

Paul forgot all about the slug until evening. When he knelt to pray, he suddenly remembered. The voice inside said, *Thou shalt not steal.* Paul squirmed. He pretended he had not heard the words. But they came again, *Thou shalt not steal, thou shalt not steal.*

The voice bothered Paul so much he decided not to pray. He jumped into bed and pulled the covers over his head. Would the covers shut out the words he didn't want to hear? No, there they were again.

Paul tossed and turned this way and that. He couldn't sleep. At last he sat up in bed in the darkness. Softly he prayed, "Dear God, I'm sorry I put the slug into Mr. Swanson's machine. I know it was wrong. Forgive me. Help me never to steal anything again. Amen."

Paul lay down. He felt better. But then it seemed as if God said, "I forgive you, Paul. But now you must pay Mr. Swanson the nickel you owe him."

I'd be ashamed to, thought Paul. *I'd have to tell him what I did . . . I can't do that.* But he knew he should do it, no matter how hard it would be.

"I'll go tell Mr. Swanson first thing in the morning," he promised. "And I'll pay him the nickel on Saturday when I get my allowance." Then he fell asleep.

In the morning he didn't forget. He asked Jesus to help him, and as soon as the store was open, Paul went in. It wasn't as hard as he thought it would be to tell what he had done. Mr. Swanson stuck his hands into his two back pockets as he listened to Paul. "Why did you come and tell me?" he asked, raising his bushy brows.

"Well, because I'm a Christian and stealing is wrong. Jesus made me sorry. He wanted me to tell you and pay you."

Mr. Swanson nodded. "I'm glad you told me. You make me wish I were a Christian too."

I'm glad I did, thought Paul.

32

Forgive Me, Please!

"Hey, Phil, may I borrow a quarter?" asked Dave. "I'll pay you back."

His big brother turned around and frowned. "Look Dave! I've decided I'm not going to lend you one more penny. Every week you borrow a nickel, a dime, or a quarter from me. And I've kept a record. Do you know how much you owe me? You owe exactly ten dollars. It's time you pay me back."

Dave looked worried. "Ten dollars! But I don't have any money, not even a dime."

"Yes, but you could pay me a dime a week out of your allowance," answered Phil.

"My allowance!" I get only thirty cents. If I give you a dime, and give a dime for Sunday School, I have only ten cents left. And you can't buy anything for a dime — have a heart," begged Dave. "It would take me forever to pay you back. Anyway, you have a job and earn more money than you need. — Can't you — well, can't you just forgive what I owe. Forgive me the ten dollars. I promise not to ask for money again?"

Phil looked at his little brother and sighed. "Ten dollars is a lot of money to forgive!" He stuck his hands in his pockets. I know it would be hard for you to pay it back but — all right, I forgive you the ten dollars."

"Thanks Phil, thanks loads," grinned Dave. "You're the best big brother I ever had."

But later that day Phil overheard something that changed his mind. He overheard Dave and his friend Ron arguing. Dave shouted, "You broke my new kite. You owe me one dollar for it."

"I'm sorry, Dave," wailed Ron. "It was an accident. Honest. I was trying to be careful. It just happened."

"I don't care," grumbled Dave. "You have to pay me a dollar for it."

"I can't," cried Ron. "I don't have a dollar."

"You will have to pay me somehow," ordered Dave. "You can borrow it from your sister or Mother or someone."

After Ron had gone home, Phil called Dave to his room. He looked at Dave for a moment. Then he said, "Dave, I've decided that you are going to have to pay me that ten dollars after all."

Dave blinked. He couldn't believe his ears.

"I overheard what you said to Ron just now," explained Phil. "And I don't think you ought to be forgiven. This morning I forgave you ten dollars. But just now you would not forgive Ron a one dollar accident." He looked at Dave sternly. "So I don't think I ought to forgive you either."

Dave hung his head. His cheeks turned pink with shame.

How he wished he had been willing to forgive Ron as Phil had been willing to forgive him!

Did you know that God tells us that we must forgive each other? God forgives *all* our sin when we believe Jesus died on the cross for us. But then He expects us to forgive others. He expects us to forgive anything anyone might do against us. He says, "Forgive one another even as God for Christ's sake has forgiven you" (Ephesians 4:32).

33

A Book of Days

Marybeth was puzzled. Among her Christmas gifts was a book from Dad. But there was not a single word or picture in it. There were only many clean white pages. Printed on its covers were the words, *Happy New Year.*

She turned the strange book over and looked at it again. She knew Dad must have a reason for giving her this gift. But she could not think what it might be.

"What kind of book is this? What's it for?" she asked. "Is it a scrapbook?"

Dad smiled at Marybeth's puzzled look. Then he explained. "In a few days it will be New Year. I gave you

this gift to remind you that the New Year is like a book. You see, each year God gives us a new book of days.

"Each day is like a clean white page — it is a page of time that God wants us to fill with good things. We must write carefully because we cannot erase what we write. And after we have written a day's thoughts, words, and deeds we cannot turn back and write them over again.

"We can write only one day at a time because we can live only one day at a time. But we do not have to do it by ourselves. If we ask Him, Jesus will guide us. And if we forget to let Jesus help us there will be blots, smears, and scratches on the pages.

"In our books of days it will help us, too, to copy from another Book. From God's own Book we may copy things like Abraham's faith, Moses' meekness, Daniel's courage, and Job's patience. And best of all, we may copy the perfect life of our Savior."

Dad paused. Marybeth looked down at her book again. Then Dad said, "When I was a boy my father gave me a book like the one I have given you. Every year since then I have often remembered that my days are pages on which God wants me to write for Him. I hope you will remember this too."

Marybeth carried the book to her room and put it on her desk with her Bible. She thought, *I didn't know I was*

*writing a book. I didn't know I was doing anything so
important. I'll prop it up where I can see it to remind me.
Then I will remember to ask Jesus to help me every day.*

Bible Words: Teach us to number our days that we
may get a heart of wisdom (Psalm 90:12).

34

Without a Pattern

The spring sun shone bright and warm. Cheerful robins
and their bird friends chirped and sang. Tim was happy
and excited. He was going to make a bird house. Dad had
given him smooth new boards and a pattern for building it.

"Be careful to follow the pattern exactly," warned Dad.
"If you don't, you will waste boards and time. — Why don't
you wait until Saturday to make it. Then I'll help you."

But Tim did not want anyone to help him. He did not
want to follow a pattern. He was sure he did not need one.
And most of all he did not want to wait.

Tim hurried away to Dad's work bench in the garage.
Soon he was busy with tools and nails.

Zzz,zzz,zzz went Dad's saw. Tim sawed the boards without
measuring or marking them. He just guessed at their size
and shape. Bang, bang, bang. He pounded nails into the
boards. But for some reason they did not fit together well
at all. The sides were crooked. And one part of the roof

was too big and the other too small. Then in his hurry he had cut the hole, the bird door, in the wrong side.

What a strange looking, crooked, bird house he made! Even the birds who came to look at it did not seem to like it when he put it up. They just flew around, chirped bird talk and went away. None of them moved in.

Tim was disappointed that no bird family moved into the new house. And Dad was disappointed too, — disappointed that Tim had been too impatient to follow the pattern.

"Next time," decided Tim staring at the crooked little house, "I'll follow a pattern and let Dad help me."

Have you ever used a pattern? Perhaps you traced one on cardboard to make a plane. Or you used one to make a kite.

There are all kinds of patterns — big ones, little ones, hard ones, easy ones, good ones, poor ones. There are pat-

terns for toys, houses, cars, airplanes, dresses, and furniture. There are even patterns we may use for our lives. Sometimes we call these examples.

But some boys and girls may be like Tim. They think they don't need a pattern. Others follow poor patterns for their lives. And some use their Dad, Mother, or teacher as their example. But the boys and girls who trust in Jesus as their Savior have the best pattern of all. Jesus said, "I have given you an example, that you should do as I have done to you." He is God's perfect pattern for our lives.

Prayer: Dear Lord Jesus, we thank You that You are our Savior. And we thank You that You are the perfect pattern for our lives. We pray that You will help us grow to be more and more like You. Amen.

35

"Leftovers"—for God

What would you think about a boy or girl who said, "I am going to wait until I am grown up before I give my heart to Jesus? Right now I want to please myself and have a good time." This is what Bud told Mr. Walters, his Sunday school teacher, one Sunday morning. Mr. Walters was disappointed but he did not show it. He knew Bud had heard his older brother say these words.

Mr. Walters had an idea. Back of his home stood a large apricot tree. And he happened to know that Bud loved fresh apricots. He waited until the apricots were juicy ripe and ready to eat. Then he filled a small basket with some of the biggest orange-cheeked apricots he could find. He carried the basket into the garage and put it on a shelf. Every day he ate an apricot or two from the basket.

One day about two weeks later he saw Bud running up the street. "Bud," he called. "Will you come here a minute?"

"Sure," answered Bud slowing down. He trotted up the drive into the garage.

"I know how you like apricots," smiled Mr. Walters.

Bud grinned and smacked his lips hungrily.

"So I picked a small basket of the nicest apricots for you two weeks ago. And here is what is left."

Bud's eyes opened wide as he looked into the basket. There were not many apricots in it. And those that were left did not look fresh and tasty. They were old and wrinkled looking.

"I ate the freshest and best apricots myself," said Mr. Walters. "But you won't mind getting only what is left, will you?"

Bud pulled his ear the way he always did when he was puzzled. He did not know what to say.

Then Mr. Walters put his hand on Bud's shoulder. "You are disappointed that I would offer you the fruit that is left after I have taken the best and freshest for myself. But isn't that the way you are treating the Lord Jesus if you do not give Him your love and life while you are young? You want to keep the best for yourself and give Him what is left."

Then Bud understood. And you will not be surprised to know that he gave his heart and life to Jesus that same day.

36

What Is My Name?

I do errands for you and for others. I never get tired or grumpy. When you give me a job to do I don't complain. Not once do I ask, "Why doesn't someone else do it?"

I seldom lose what you trust to me. I will go wherever you want me to go — on short trips or long ones. I won't cost you much money — not more than a candy bar or two.

If you wish I'll travel to India for you. Or I'll go to Africa, Alaska, or Australia. I'll deliver what you give me to places near or far.

To serve you I may sail the ocean in a big ship. Or speed through the sky in a silver plane. Sometimes I may go by bicycle, truck, or train. I may even plod along on a donkey's back. Or I may sway on a camel's bumps, or be carried by a man.

I'm not very large and there are many of me. You will find me and my friends busy in every country. We work together to serve you. We follow certain rules and each one of us does his part. We always try to stick to our job until it's done.

When I'm given an errand to do I'm put in a box. The box is red, white, and blue. Then I'm taken out of the box and put into a sack. I ride in a truck to a certain building. There I get set for my trip, near or far.

Do you know who I am? Shall I tell you what I look like? Sometimes I wear a face like Abraham Lincoln or Thomas Jefferson. But other times I wear the face of a woman. Or I look like a building or a plane. My name is Postage Stamp.

In some ways I'm like you.

Some one made me.

You were made by God.

I was made to serve others.

God made you to serve Him.

I deliver messages.

If you trust in the Lord Jesus He wants you to deliver a message too. He says, "Go into all the world and tell the gospel to everyone."

I follow rules.

God has rules for you to follow. They are in His Word.

"Whatever you do, do it with all your hearts for the Lord . . . You are serving Christ, the Master."

—Colossians 3:23a, 24a

37

Jailed

It was a shivery November day in 1660. Preacher John
Bunyan was going to do what he had been warned not to do.
He was going to preach. Some men had cautioned him,
"If you preach again you will be arrested."

But Preacher Bunyan was not afraid. He paid no attention to the warning. Off he hurried to a little meeting-house
a few miles away. Gathered there were happy Christians who
had invited him to preach for them. Just as John stood up in
the meeting and began to pray, something happened. In
walked the constable and his men. They had come to
arrest him and take him to jail.

Away John Bunyan was marched to Bedford prison. Why
was he jailed for preaching? In those days in England
there was to be no preaching except in the one big church.

But John and many other people didn't agree. They believed Christians should be allowed to meet where they pleased and hear the minister they chose.

So the big church decided to jail ministers like John Bunyan. That, they thought, would stop such preaching. But it did not stop John Bunyan. If he couldn't preach outside of prison, he would preach inside. Gladly the other prisoners listened as he taught them God's Word. And soon he had a little church group in Bedford jail.

One day some officers visited Bunyan in prison. "You may go free," they said, "if you only will promise not to preach anymore."

"No," replied John, "I will make no such promise. For if you let me out of jail today, I will preach again tomorrow. That is what God wants me to do. I will obey Him, not you."

The officers became very angry. They scolded John and made fun of him. "We will throw you out of England," they threatened, "or we will stretch your neck." That meant they might even hang him. But nothing they said or did could change John's mind. He would not promise not to preach again.

John was imprisoned most of the time for twelve years to keep him from preaching. Yet he found a way to preach to people outside of Bedford jail. Can you think how?

Over and over John had been reading his Bible until his head and heart were filled with its words. Then he began to write books and tracts. These were printed by his friends. People in many towns bought and read them. The last book John wrote in jail was called *Pilgrim's Progress*. All over England people read this book and liked it. Soon men, women, and children in France, Holland, Germany, and America were reading it too. *Pilgrim's Progress* became one of the world's best-known books.

It is almost 300 years since John Bunyan wrote this famous book. But boys and girls and men and women are still reading it.

So the men who tried to keep John Bunyan from preaching to a few really helped him preach to millions through the books he wrote in prison. God turned all the wrong they planned against him to good. For God has promised that "all things work together for good to them that love God."

38

How Long the Way?

"Am I ever tired," sighed Jeff as he flopped down on the grass and leaned against a tree.

"Me, too," groaned Doug, sprawling on the grass.

It was a warm Saturday afternoon. Jeff, Doug, and seven other boys were on a hike with their Sunday school teacher, Mr. George.

Jeff took off his shoe and shook it. Why, he wondered, do I always get stones in my shoes when I walk?

"I bet we walked ten miles," said Doug.

"Ten miles!" scoffed Jeff. "I bet it was at least fifteen."

The friendly argument went on. One boy said they walked only two miles, another thought it was twelve. Someone else was sure it was twenty. But Mr. George smiled and said, "I think you are all wrong." He pulled a little round thing that looked like a pocket-watch out of his pocket and looked at it a moment. Then he said, "We have walked five and a half miles."

"You mean that little thing can tell how far we've walked?" asked Jeff amazed.

"What is it? How can it do that?"

"Yes," answered Mr. George, "this instrument tells how far we have hiked. It is a pedometer."

The curious boys crowded close to look at it as Mr. George held it up for them to see.

"This morning just before we started out I set it and put it in my pocket," he explained. "Every time I took a step the hand on this dial moved forward. You see, each step

I took shook the pedometer. The pedometer counted the times I put my feet down."

Mr. George passed the instrument to the boys so they could get a better look at it.

"Boy, that's keen," commented Doug. "I'd like a pe-pe- a thing like that too."

"A pedometer, Doug," said Mr. George helpfully.

Jeff shook his head, "How about that? You could carry it all day and then at night you'd know how far you'd walked."

"And you would know how tired you should be," added Mr. George.

"Could I borrow it for a whole day sometime?" begged Jeff.

"Oh, I think that could be arranged," replied Mr. George. He was always ready to do things for the boys. "I could set it for you and explain how to read it. Of course, it is a delicate instrument. You couldn't play rough games while you carried it."

"Does a pe-pe- pedometer cost very much?" asked Doug. "Maybe we could save enough money to buy one for ourselves."

"You could probably get one for about five dollars," answered Mr. George. He looked thoughtful. "It is an interesting instrument. You would surely have a lot of fun with it on your hikes. But you know, I can think of something that's a lot more important for boys to Remember, a pedometer can only tell you hc walked. It can't tell you where you are goin, can't tell you how to get where you want to go. But . is something that can tell you where you have come from, where you are going in life, and even the way to the place you want to go."

The boys' eyes were big and round with surprise. What kind of an "instrument" could do all that? They were puzzled.

"It is nice to have a pedometer," continued Mr. George, "yet I don't use it every often. But this other thing I use every day. I have it with me now, too."

Mr. George stopped. He reached into the big, bulging pocket of his plaid shirt and pulled out a — yes, a pocket Bible.

The boys relaxed. They thought, *We should have guessed what it was!*

1. What does the Bible tell us about who made us?

2. What does the Bible say about two ways in which people walk?

3. If someone should ask you the way to heaven, what would you tell him?

If you don't know the answers to these questions you can find them in the Bible.

1. Read Genesis 1:27 and John 1:3.
2. Look up Matthew 7:13-14.
3. Read and think about John 14:6.

Prayer: Dear heavenly Father, I thank You for the Bible. I thank You that it tells us about Jesus who is the way to heaven. Help me to trust in Him as my Savior. Amen.

39

Escape

Tramp — tramp — tramp. The prison guards' footsteps sounded loud in the quiet night. Soldier Winston held his breath and waited until the guards had marched by his hiding place. Then he bent low and dashed to the prison wall.

Jumping on a ledge, he stretched tall and grabbed hold of the top of the wall. With a mighty pull, he went up and over. But his coat caught in the metal edging. And not far from him he could hear the guards talking. He had to escape before they returned. Frantically he tugged at his coat. Suddenly it came loose and he dropped down on the other side of the wall — free!

But Soldier Winston was alone in enemy territory in Africa. He was three hundred miles away from the English army to which he belonged. Scattered around the countryside were enemy soldiers, and he had no map to help him find his way. He did not dare to ask anyone directions, for he could not speak their language.

What should he do? Where should he go? *I'll follow the railroad,* he decided. *Perhaps a train will come this way shortly.*

Trudging along mile after mile, Winston became tired. At last a train rattled up the tracks behind him. As it was passing, he took a chance and jumped aboard. He almost missed and landed under the wheels, but somehow he held fast and crawled into one of the cars. Among empty, dusty coal sacks, weary Winston curled up and slept.

Just before dawn he awoke. *I must get off the train before it is day,* he thought, *or I'll be seen and caught.* He climbed over the side of the car and took a big leap, landing safely in a heap on the ground. Quickly he scrambled to his feet and looked around. Now for a hiding place. Nearby was just the place — some hills. He ran to them and hid there the long, hot day. How thirsty he got — and lonely too! His only company was a hungry-looking vulture circling around and around above him in the burning sky.

At last night came. Winston was tired, hungry, and

afraid. He tried to cheer himself up, but it didn't do any good. He prayed hard that God would help and guide him, and he felt better.

In the darkness he tramped along the railroad again, but no train came. Finally, at a certain place he saw some lighted European-style houses. Who lived in them? Friendly people or enemies? Winston didn't know. But one thing was sure. He was too tired to go any further. He went and knocked at the first door he came to.

A gruff voice answered from inside. The door rattled and was jerked open by a man with a gun in his hand. "Who are you and what do you want?" asked the man. Winston started to explain. The man looked at him sharply. "Come in," he ordered. He sat down and laid his gun on the table.

"I'll tell you the truth," said Winston bravely. "I am a British soldier, a prisoner of war who has escaped."

The man did not say a word. Slowly he stood, walked to the door, and locked it. *What now?* wondered Winston. *Am I going to be arrested, or shot, or . . .?*

Then a surprising thing happened. The man turned and held out his hand to Winston. "Thank God you have come here," he said earnestly. "This is the only house for twenty miles where you are safe. At any other you would have been turned over to the enemy. Like you, we are British. We will get you back to your group."

Winston Churchill felt like shouting for joy. God had guided him! He had escaped!

This exciting story of Winston Churchill's escape reminds me of an enemy we have — one who wants to keep us prisoners of sin. And we can never, never free ourselves. So our Saviour allowed Himself to be taken prisoner and to die in our place that we might be free from the guilt and power of sin, and so we also have entered a door into the House of God who is our friend and who protects and saves us.

40

The Game Girl

It was evening in Dundee, Scotland. A slim girl hurried along a narrow, dark street in the slums. Suddenly a group of young hoodlums jumped out at her. Grinning, they formed a circle and fenced her in. "We'll take care of you if you don't leave us alone," they warned.

The girl was afraid. But she did not show it. She looked at the boys with quiet eyes and breathed a prayer for God's help.

"You can do what you like," she answered in a soft voice. "I will not give up."

"All right," shouted the big boy who was the leader. "Here goes."

From his pocket the boy pulled a cord, to which a heavy lump of lead was tied. Round and round he began to whirl the lead. Nearer and nearer to the girl's head he brought it.

The girl stood straight and calm. Amazed at her courage the other hoodlums watched breathlessly. The heavy lead swished by the girl's forehead. She did not even flinch. She waited coolly for the lead to strike her and knock her down. Suddenly the big boy jerked the cord. The weight crashed to the street.

"She's game, boys," he exclaimed in wonder and admiration.

The brave girl had won. But the rough boys were good losers. Like lambs they followed her into the nearby mission building and sat down in her Bible class. To their surprise they listened and liked what they heard. Never again did the boys wish to trouble Mary Slessor, the "game" girl with the soft voice.

Why had they tried to frighten Mary? Because she was the Sunday school teacher at the new mission in the slums where they lived. They wanted her to leave them alone. They did not want her to bother them about going to Sunday school or church. When Mary first came, they made loud noises to annoy her. Then they had thrown stones and mud at her. When that did not stop her, they had tried to scare her away. But instead they became her faithful friends. Best of all, the leader of the gang and the worst boys in it became friends of the Lord Jesus.

Not long after this Mary was in still greater danger. She became a missionary in the jungles of Africa. She tramped through dark forests where elephants, rhinoceroses, and leopards prowled. Up and down rivers filled with crocodiles, snakes, and hippopotamuses she canoed.

Mary made her home in mud-thatched huts among murderers and thieves. Often she was in danger. Always she trusted the Lord to help her. Her loving ways, her soft voice, and her bravery surprised the wild forest people. Soon they, too, listened to what she had come to tell them

— the good news about the Lord Jesus. Many of them believed in Him as their Saviour and became happy Christians.

Mary Slessor, the brave little missionary to Calabar, died and was buried in Africa.

41

The Word-Beggar

Years ago on a South Sea island lived a poor farmer named Buteve who had no hands or feet. A disease the islanders called *kokavi* had eaten them away. But Buteve did not complain. Cheerfully he walked about his fields on his knees. With the stumps of his arms he worked the ground, planted crops and weeded them. By long hours of hard work he grew food for his little family.

One evening John Williams, the missionary on this island, strolled along the path near Buteve's home. The minute the poor farmer saw the missionary coming he slid off the seat by his hut. Slowly he hobbled toward Mr. Williams and called, "Welcome, servant of God, who has brought Jesus' light to this dark island. We are in debt to you for bringing us the word of salvation."

Mr. Williams stopped and stared in surprise. He had never seen this man before. "What do you know about the word of salvation?" he asked the farmer.

Buteve's dark eyes shone. "I know Jesus came into the world to save sinners. And I know He is God's Son who died painfully on a cross to pay for men's sins so they might go to happiness in the skies."

Mr. Williams was puzzled and more surprised than ever. How did the farmer who had no books, who could not read, and who never came to church know these things? The missionary tested him by asking "Will every one go to heaven?"

The farmer shook his head. "Of course not! Only those who believe in Jesus, who throw away their sin, and who pray to God."

"Do you pray?" asked Mr. Williams.

"Oh, yes," nodded Buteve. "I pray often as I weed my ground and plant my fields. Always three times a day I pray, besides praying with my family every morning and evening."

"What do you say when you pray?"

"I say, 'O Lord, I am a great sinner. May Jesus take my sins away by His blood. Give me Jesus' goodness and give me the good spirit of Jesus to teach me and to make my heart good. Make me a man of Jesus, and take me to heaven when I die.' "

"That is fine," said Mr. Williams. "But where did you learn about Jesus?"

"Why, from you," smiled the farmer. "You brought this news."

"True," agreed the missionary. "But I have never seen you before. So how did you hear about these things?"

"As the people come from your meetings I sit here by this path and beg. I beg words of them. One tells me some of your words. Another tells me other words and I collect all these words in my heart. Then I think about them and pray to God to make me know what they mean. So I understand a little about Jesus."

How delighted Mr. Williams was to meet the word-beggar! Gladly he sat down to visit with Buteve and to give him more words to collect in his heart. Afterward the missionary often went to see the happy farmer to take him still more words of Jesus.

42

Why Karjarnak Wept

Years ago, in a little hut in Greenland, a missionary sat at a table. In front of him lay a book and some sheets of paper. The missionary stared at a page in the book for a while, then carefully wrote on one of the sheets of paper. After a minute he looked in the book again and wrote down a few more words. What was he doing? For hours and days he had been translating the Gospel of John into the language of the people in that area.

Suddenly someone pounded loudly on the door of his hut. The door flew open and in stomped the wicked chieftain, Karjarnak. He had come down from the mountains to pay the missionary a visit.

Karjarnak, who could not read or write, looked at the book and papers on the table. "What you do?" he asked, pointing at them.

"I'm making marks on these papers," explained the missionary holding up a sheet. "These marks are words and the words tell a wonderful story."

The chieftain's eyes gleamed, "What story do the words tell?"

"Sit down," invited the missionary. "I'll read it to you."

Slowly the missionary read the story of Jesus' death on the cross. The chieftain leaned forward on his stool listening so closely he scarcely seemed to breathe. When the missionary stopped reading, the chieftain asked, "What has this man Jesus done? Has he robbed or murdered someone?"

The missionary shook his head. "No, he never robbed or murdered anyone."

"Then why must he suffer? Why does he die?"

"This man has done nothing wrong, but Karjarnak has," said the missionary. "This man has never robbed anyone, but Karjarnak has often robbed people. This man has never murdered anyone, but Karjarnak has. But because the man loves Karjarnak He suffered so that Karjarnak might not suffer. He died that Karjarnak might not die."

"Tell me the story again," begged the astonished chieftain.

The missionary read it another time.

Big tears glistened in Karjarnak's eyes and rolled down his rough cheeks. To think that someone should suffer and die in his place for his wickedness! "Tell me more about this man," he pleaded.

At last Karjarnak thanked the missionary and said goodbye. He hurried back to the mountains to tell his people the wonderful story of Jesus. And from that day Karjarnak was a new man.

43

Crooked Arm's Bravest Deed

Crooked Arm was a cunning Indian warrior who liked nothing better than to make war. Through his bravery he had become the proud, powerful chief of the Cree tribe.

In a battle with the Blackfoot Indians his arm had been badly cut. And when it healed it was stiff and crooked.

So his people called him Maskepetoom, which means "Crooked Arm."

Brave Maskepetoom had only one son, whom he loved very much. One day he sent his son with another warrior to a green valley where the tribe's horses were kept. They were to look after the horses. But the warrior was dishonest. He killed Crooked Arm's son and sold the horses for much money. Then he returned to camp and told the chief that his son had fallen from a high cliff and been killed. He said that the horses had all run away.

Somehow Chief Crooked Arm discovered what had really happened. Fierce anger filled his heart and he vowed to kill the lying warrior.

But in those days a missionary named George McDougal visited the Indians. In the evening he sat with them around their camp fire talking to them about Jesus. He told them of God's great love for Indians. He explained that God had sent His Son to die for their sins. Then he described how Jesus had died on the cross and how Jesus prayed for the cruel men who nailed Him there, saying, "Father forgive them, for they know not what they do."

"God will forgive your sins if you trust in Jesus as your Savior," said Mr. McDougal. "But then you must forgive others as God forgives you. Jesus said, 'If you will not forgive other people, neither will your heavenly Father forgive you.'" Chief Crooked Arm listened carefully. He thought much about these words.

The next day the missionary rode with the Chief and his warriors out on the prairie. As they rode along they saw another group of Indians. Among them was the warrior who had killed the Chief's son. The eagle eyes of Crooked Arm spotted the warrior. Quickly he pulled his tomahawk from his belt and rode faster. When he came face to face with the warrior he stopped his horse and sat straight and tall. Silently he stared at the man. Then slowly he put his tomahawk back in his belt and began to speak.

"You killed my son," he said sternly. "You deserve to die. I trusted you and gave you the honor of helping my son. But you killed him. By the laws of all Indians you should die.

"But last evening the white man told us about the Great Spirit. He said that if we expect the Great Spirit to forgive us we must forgive others. We must even forgive our enemies." The Chief's voice trembled. "You are my worst enemy. But as I hope the Great Spirit will forgive me, I now freely forgive you."

Then the brave Chief bowed over his horse's neck and wept. To forgive this enemy was the hardest thing he had ever done. It was his bravest deed.

So proud Chief Maskepetoom became a humble follower of Jesus. He did not make war anymore. Instead He learned to read the Bible in the Cree language. And he began to tell others about Jesus. He even went to tell his enemies, the Blackfeet, about the Savior. He used to go to them with hate in his heart and a tomahawk in his hand. Now he went to them with love in his heart and a Bible in his hand.

"If a man is in Christ he becomes a new person" (II Corinthians 5:17).

44

Forgetful Lucy

"Lucy," called Mother, "Lucy, where are you?"

"Here," answered Lucy popping her head out of the door of her room.

"Please watch Bobby for me," said Mother. "I must go see Mrs. Vandenberg a few minutes before we go down town."

Ten-year-old Lucy nodded.

"Now watch him every minute," warned Mother. "Don't let him out of your sight."

"I won't," promised Lucy cheerfully.

Lucy is so forgetful and careless, thought Mother as she hurried to Mrs. Vandenberg's. *I don't know if I should have left Bobby with her . . . But it's only for a few minutes.*

"Come, Bobby," said Lucy when Mother was gone. "We'll look at your picture storybook." Little Bobby loved story-books. Up onto the sofa he scrambled and wriggled close to

Lucy. Slowly she turned the pages of his book. "See," Bobby said and put his plump forefinger on each picture. What fun, he thought, it was to point at the pictures and chatter about them!

Just then the phone rang. It was Lucy's friend, Sylvia, with exciting news about the party their school class was planning. As Lucy talked with Sylvia, she kept an eye on Bobby. At first he sat quietly looking at his book. Soon he got up and wandered into the kitchen. Lucy couldn't see him but she heard him.

But Bobby was scarcely out of sight before Lucy forgot all about him. It seemed like only a minute later that Mother came in the front door. When Lucy saw her mother she quickly said good-bye to Sylvia. She gasped and put her hand over her mouth. — *Bobby* — she had forgotten all about him.

"Where's Bobby?" asked Mother looking around.

"In the kitchen," answered Lucy dashing to get him. But Bobby wasn't in the kitchen or any other room. He wasn't in the backyard either. Lucy ran to the front of the house and looked up and down the sidewalk. She didn't see him anywhere. Suddenly she had a fluttery, scared feeling in her stomach. What if Bobby had gotten lost? Or hurt, or . . .?

Mother came out the front door looking concerned. "Lucy," she sighed sadly. "I told you to watch Bobby *every* minute."

"I know, Mother, and I meant to. But when Sylvia called I forgot."

"Well, you go looking and calling on the other side of the street," ordered Mother. "I'll look on this side."

Off Lucy ran. She looked everywhere she thought Bobby might be. And she asked everyone she met if they had seen him. At last one man said he'd seen a little fellow in the next block. Lucy ran across busy Lincoln Avenue. She

113

was almost crying she was so worried. There was no sign of Bobby anywhere.

But just when she was ready to give up and run back to Mother she heard a sound. A voice called, "Loothy." She whirled around. Close to the street was Bobby peeking from behind a big tree.

Lucy grabbed and hugged him tight. She'd never been so glad to see him in her life. "Oh, Bobby, why did you run away?" she wailed. "And why do I always forget?" She took his hand and led him home as fast as his little legs could go. On the way they met Mother. How happy she was to see them both!

As they got into the car to go downtown, Lucy was very quiet. To think that little Bobby had crossed big, busy Lincoln Avenue all by himself! He could have been hurt or even killed!

"Oh, Mother," said Lucy earnestly. "If something had happened to Bobby it would have been all my fault . . . . I don't think I'll ever be so forgetful again."

"No, I don't think you will be either," agreed Mother. For at last Lucy was truly sorry.

45

A Careless Master

Storm clouds darkened the summer sky as the Benson family was eating their dinner. Through the window Ricky saw a flash of lightning. "Boy, there's going to be a real storm," he announced.

"Oh, that reminds me," said Mother, "Where's Rolf?" Rolf was the Benson's dog. And Rolf did not like thunderstorms.

Ricky jumped. "I forgot — I forgot all about Rolf," he said, starting to leave the table. "I've got to go and get him right away — before the storm."

"Just a minute, Son," said Dad.

"But Dad," wailed Ricky, "Rolf is at the playground. I told him to guard my bat and glove while I ran to Dale's house. And then — I forgot all about him. He's still out there watching my stuff. He's been there a couple of hours. I've got to go get him."

"Finish your dinner first," suggested Dad.

"But Dad, the storm — you know how Rolf is scared of

lightning and thunder. Besides, he'll get soaked, and so will my bat and glove."

"We will finish our dinner," said Dad, "Then I'll drive you to the playground to get Rolf."

Ricky nodded. He ate the rest of his dinner quickly. Poor Rolf. Ricky could just see him sitting all alone in the middle of the playground — waiting obediently.

Lightning flashed. Thunder rumbled and rolled. A strong wind bent the poplar trees. Any minute rain would pour down. —There! The first big drops splashed against the window.

"Can't we go now?" asked Ricky impatiently.

Dad took his last bite of dessert and put down his napkin. "All right," he smiled. "Let's go."

He and Ricky dashed to the garage and jumped into the car. Carefully Dad backed the car out the driveway and turned down the street. In a few minutes they were at the playground. By that time the rain had begun to pour down. Dad pulled up to the curb. Ricky hopped out of the car and ran to get his bat and glove. "Here, Rolf! Here, Rolf!" he called as he ran. Rolf came running to meet him, bark-

ing and wagging his tail. Ricky grabbed his bat and glove. Together they raced to the car and jumped in.

Inside the car, Rolf gave himself a happy shake. Water showered Ricky and Dad. Dad laughed and got out his handkerchief to wipe away the drops. Rolf rubbed his wet head against Ricky.

"I'm sorry I forgot you, fella'," murmured Ricky, patting Rolf's head. "You're a good dog." Rolf wriggled with pleasure.

"You do what I tell you, don't you? You even guarded my stuff in the storm."

Rolf made happy noises and licked his master's cheek with his long pink tongue.

"I guess Rolf is a pretty special dog, isn't he, Dad? He likes to do what I tell him. See how pleased he looks?"

Dad drove slowly. "Yes, and I think his obedience is a lesson to us, Ricky. If he is so glad to obey a careless master — how much more should we be glad to obey our wise heavenly Master."

Ricky patted Rolf again as Dad turned up their street and then into their driveway. *I wish I did obey Jesus as well as Rolf does me,* thought Ricky.

> Trust and obey
> For there is no other way
> To be happy in Jesus
> But to trust and obey.

117

46

Your Move

Did you ever play checkers?

You think it looks like a stupid game?

Well, I used to think it was stupid, too. But I sure don't any more.

One day after Grandpa came to live with us, he said, "Arthur, how about taking some exercise with me?" His blue eyes twinkled.

"Sure," I said, being polite. I wondered what kind of exercise he'd take. Grandpa is old. He can't even walk well anymore.

Grandpa turned, tottered off to his room, and came

back with this box and board. When he opened the board, I groaned to myself — it was a checkerboard! But I just said, "I thought you wanted to take some exercise, Grandpa."

His little white beard and moustache stretched with his smile. "I do. I want to exercise my mind. And I don't know any better way than to play checkers. It's the game to exercise your 'mind-muscles.' Come. I'll show you."

I didn't want to play, but what could I do? I had said I would. I thought I'd just play with him this once to please him.

Grandpa showed me a few special moves and tricks. And we played a game. Then he showed me a few more and we played another. Before I knew it we'd played a whole string of games. And it was fun — not a bit stupid. Grandpa wasn't joking when he said it was exercise. I never thought so hard before.

So Grandpa and I have been exercising together almost every day. Grandpa doesn't know it, but a few weeks ago I borrowed a book on checkers from the library. I've been studying it secretly. I've wanted to see if I could learn some moves he doesn't know. But he knows every one I've tried so far. He's sharp.

That book I borrowed says there are so many different moves you could never use all of them. How about that! And you know what else? The Pharaohs, the kings who ruled Egypt in Bible times, used to play checkers. So did the Greeks and Romans. Think of playing a game those people long ago played!

Wouldn't you like to learn it, too? Grandpa says checkers will keep me from having a lazy, flabby mind. He says God wants us to have strong minds and bodies to serve Him.

47

Until Then

Mary Lou loved to climb trees, run, jump rope, and ride bicycle. But her sister, Pam, never did any of these things with her. She just watched. For she was crippled. She had thin, weak legs and crooked feet. Only by wearing heavy braces and using crutches could she walk at all. Clack — clack — clack — sounded Pam's braces on the floor with each slow step. Thump—slide—thump—slide whispered her rubber-tipped crutches wherever she went.

Each morning Mother and Mary Lou fastened Pam's stiff brace straps for her. Evenings Pam tried to pick the strap buckles open herself. And over-night she wanted the clumsy braces and crutches to lie across the bottom of her bed. "My other legs must rest, too," she said.

Sometimes Mary Lou wished Pam could run and jump with her. She dreamed about all the fun they could have together.

"Oh, Mother, I wish Pam had good legs, too," she sighed one evening. "I just don't see why she doesn't."

Mother looked up from sewing a button on Mary Lou's nightie. She tipped her head to the side, the way she did when she was thinking.

"Well, do you remember the story of how Adam and Eve disobeyed God at the beginning of the world?"

"Mm-m," answered Mary Lou untying her shoes.

"When Adam and Eve disobeyed God, sin, sickness, and sorrow came into the world," explained Mother. "Since then none of us has a pure heart or a perfect body. All of us are sinful. All of us get sick sometimes and have pain. And

some people are even blind, or deaf, or have sick minds, or are lame or crippled like Pam and like the little boy in the next block." Mother paused while Mary Lou pulled off her socks.

"But because God loves us He sent Jesus to die for our sin so we can be forgiven when we believe in Him. And then one day He will also give us sinless hearts and perfect bodies."

"I know when that will happen," smiled Mary Lou bouncing gently on her bed. "When we go to heaven to be with Jesus."

Mother's nimble fingers made a knot in the thread under the button she had sewed fast. Snip went her scissors, and the nightie was ready for Mary Lou to wear.

"Pam can't scamper around like you," continued Mother. "But she can love Jesus and praise and serve Him. For God has given her sharp eyes and ears. And He has given her a good mind. Why, she is only five and look how she reads, writes, and draws already.

"She's smart," nodded Mary Lou proudly.

"Of course Pam often wishes she could run and play with you. And sometimes she feels discouraged. But she is learning to be content with what she has. And I think she is happier than many boys and girls I know who are healthier and stronger than she."

Prayer: Dear Lord Jesus, we thank You that one day we may be where there is no sin or suffering. Until then help us to be contented and to praise and serve You with whatever we have. Amen.

48

The Happy Gardeners

It was a warm spring day. Amy and Scotty were as busy as beavers. First they went to the garage and got their red wheelbarrow, into which they loaded their toy shovel, rake, and hoe. Then Scotty pushed it to the garden, while Amy ran to get the garden seeds from the shelf in the kitchen where Dad had put them.

Together they dug, raked, hoed, and sowed. What fun they had scattering the different kinds of tiny seeds and covering them up. They stuck each empty seed envelope on a stick the way Dad did to mark where the seeds had been sown.

Amy giggled, "Won't Dad be surprised? We will have all his seeds planted for him."

Scotty sat back on his heels. He pushed his hair out of his eyes and looked around proudly. Then he clawed more holes in the ground and Amy dropped the seeds from the last envelope in. They quickly tossed their tools into the wheelbarrow and pushed it back to the garage. Laughing, they ran to tell Mother about their surprise for Dad.

"Mother, come and see what we did," they called. When Mother came to look, they could see that she was very surprised, too.

"Oh," she said slowly, "how pleased Dad will be that you wanted to help him and that you were willing to work so hard. . . . I think I'll have to reward such hard-working gardeners with nice cool glasses of chocolate milk."

Feeling proud and pleased, Amy and Scotty raced to

the kitchen. And as they sipped their chocolate, Mother looked out the window at the crowded little garden her happy gardeners had made. Turning to Amy and Scotty she said, "It's nice that you wanted to help Dad. He will be glad. But you know, because you didn't wait for him to tell you how, you forgot some of the rules of planting."

"We did?" chorused the two. "But we tried to be real careful," said Amy. "What did we forget?"

"Well, you forgot that not all seeds get planted at the same time. And you forgot to leave room for them to grow and for us to hoe around them," answered Mother.

"Oh," said Amy looking dismayed. "I should have thought about that."

"Don't worry," said Mother cheerfully. "Dad will buy us new seeds and we can do it over. But let your mistake remind us what happens if we don't think about how or what we sow in our other garden — the garden of hearts. Sometimes we forget to let our heavenly Father guide and help us, don't we? Then we plant unwisely and are sorry."

Prayer: Dear Lord Jesus, sow seeds of trust in You in the garden of our hearts while it is springtime. Plant also seeds of love, obedience, truth, and goodness and make them grow. Amen.

49

Dan's Penalty

Dan stuck his cold, fidgety hands into his back pockets. He took a deep breath and stood tall and straight. He looked up at Judge Scott seated in a big chair between two flags. Dan knew the judge well. He was his Sunday school teacher. But this wasn't Sunday school. It was the traffic court. How solemn and stern Judge Scott looked in his black robe! Dan shifted his feet uneasily. He was scared.

"Now, Dan," said Judge Scott kindly, "Suppose you tell me exactly what happened."

Dan swallowed. "Well, sir, I was riding down Madison Street on my bike. And there was this traffic light — you know the one at Madison and High. It turned red just as I got to the corner. And . . . well, I-I thought I could still get through before the cars started. Then it happened. A big car was coming right at me. I swerved hard to get out of the way. I guess the man tried to miss me, too. Anyway, his car hit another car instead of me."

Dan stopped and cleared his throat. "I know it was wrong and I'm awfully sorry. I'll sure never do it again."

Judge Scott was silent a moment. He looked thoughtful. "You know, Dan, because you broke a law you caused an accident. Of course, we are thankful no one was hurt. But I have no choice; I must fine you for going through the red light and causing the accident. Your fine is fifteen dollars."

"Fifteen dollars!" Dan gasped and turned pale. "Fifteen dollars!" *What'll I do?* he wondered frantically. *I don't even have one dollar. How can I ever pay fifteen?*

Judge Scott seemed to know what Dan was thinking. "I know you don't have the money," he said, "But that is the penalty and it must be paid."

Slowly the judge got up from his chair. "Come, I will go with you to the window where fines are paid," he said.

Soon they stood in front of a window. Then the judge handed the man there a slip of paper and said, "This is Dan Johnson. He owes fifteen dollars for riding his bike through a red light and causing an accident. But he can't pay it. So," the Judge paused, pushed his robe back, reached in his pocket, and took out a worn billfold, "I am going to pay his fine for him."

Dan blinked glad tears back. "Tha-thank you Judge Scott," he stammered. "Thank you very much."

The judge put his hand on Dan's shoulder and walked to the door with him. He said, "Dan, let this remind you of a much greater penalty Someone has paid for you."

Dan looked puzzled.

The Judge continued, "Let it remind you how God gave His Son to die for us. We have broken His holy laws and could not pay the penalty. But because God loves us, He sent Jesus to pay it for us.

50

Bill's Gift

With an armful of newspapers Bill stood on his favorite corner. *"Evening Post! Evening Post!"* he called loudly. "Buy your *Post* here. Buy your *Post* here." Bill hoped lots of people on their way home from work would stop and buy his papers. With the money he earned he hoped to buy a telescope. He'd seen the very one he wanted pictured in a catalogue. Already he had $7.50 in his savings bank toward it.

But then something happened. On Sunday Bill's Sunday school classmates were buzzing with ideas and excitement. They were getting ready for Christmas — Christmas in October! In their little church the last Sunday in October was Missionary-Christmas Sunday. Everyone brought gifts the missionaries needed for their work. The gifts were brought in October so they could be mailed early. That way they would be sure to reach the faraway missionaries in time for Christmas.

Some boys and girls planned to bring warm clothing for poor children in Alaska. Some were making Bible-story picture books for children in a missionary hospital in South America. Others were saving money to help buy medicine for lepers in India.

What will I bring? wondered Bill. He thought and prayed about it. Then he had an idea. He told his teacher, Mr. Dixon, his idea. "Wonderful!" exclaimed Mr. Dixon. "I think I know where you can get what you want." Bill was excited.

But his gift would cost money. The $7.50 toward his telescope was all he had. Should he use a tenth of it? Or half? Or . . . ? Mr. Dixon said, "Remember God's gift when you give to others."

The next day Bill emptied his bank. With all the telescope money in his pocket he hurried to the store Mr. Dixon had told him about.

"Do you have Spanish Bibles?" he asked the clerk breathlessly. "How much would five cost?"

"Yes, we have Spanish Bibles," answered the clerk. "Let's see, five would cost $7.50."

"$7.50!" stammered Bill. He put his hand into his pocket and held onto his money. He hadn't thought of giving up *all* his telescope money. *I could buy only one or two Bibles,* he thought. *That would be enough, wouldn't it? . . . But I'd like to give five.* He shifted from one foot to the other.

"I'll take . . . f-f-five," he said swallowing bravely. Then he explained to the clerk what he was going to do with the Bibles.

"Well," smiled the clerk, "since this is such a special gift, I think I can give you six Bibles for your money instead of five. How would you like that?"

"That'd be swell," beamed Bill.

At last it was Missionary-Christmas Sunday. One by one the children took their gifts to the front of the church. They laid them on a big table in front of a cross and told whom the gifts were for. The following week all the gifts were packed and mailed to the missionaries.

Weeks later, Bill received a letter from the missionary in Guatemala. "Dear Bill," the missionary wrote, "How surprised we were to receive your gift of six Spanish Bibles. We will give them to our six new pupils at the mission school. They will be so happy to have Bibles of their very own. Isn't it thrilling that we should have six new pupils who need Bibles just when your gift came? God knew all about it and put it into your heart to give Bibles. We thank Him and you for them."

How glad I am, thought Bill, *that I gave all my telescope money for the Bibles!*

51

More Important than Arithmetic

The boys of Riverton School were gathered in noisy groups on the playground. Some were playing games; others were talking or yelling. When the bell rang, several boys raced toward the school entrance. The rest were surprised to see a Negro boy coming up the walk.

As the Negro boy drew near, the boys became silent. "Hi," greeted the boy shyly. No one answered until he had

passed and started up the steps. Then a boy called out, "Hi, Brownie." And a few more chimed in impishly, "Hi, Brownie."

George — that was the Negro boy's name — gritted his teeth and ran into the building. It was a miserable morning for him. The boys stared at him. Silly girls looked at him and whispered and giggled. And again during recess the same boy called, "Hi, Brownie," and laughed at him.

George clenched his fists, "My name's George, you stupid paleface. Stop calling me Brownie or I'll. . . ."

"O.K, Brownie," grinned the boy with a so-what-will-you-do-about-it look.

Angrily George started for him. But the bell rang, and everyone ran, laughing, back into the building.

After recess George had to go to take some tests in the principal's office. And while he was gone from the class-room, the teacher, Miss Stephens, said, "We'll skip our arithmetic assignment today. We must find the answer to a more important problem."

Pleased, the boys rolled their eyes and cheered quietly. One girl whispered, "Yippee!" Others pretended to clap their hands.

Miss Stephens waited until all the pupils gave her their full attention. "This morning," she began, "and during recess some of you forgot something important." The room became very still. "Do you know what you forgot?" Miss Stephens looked around questioningly.

One girl raised her hand. "I think I know. You mean

we forgot to be kind to the new boy. I guess we forgot because — well, you know, because he's different — he's a Negro. We never had a Negro in our class before."

Miss Stephens nodded. "It was rude to stare at George and to whisper and giggle about him. But, worst of all, some of you called him *Brownie*. How would you like to have been welcomed to a new place so unkindly?"

The children looked ashamed and squirmed in their seats.

"It was very wrong to tease George about the color of his skin," continued Miss Stephens. "Who can tell me why?" The boys and girls thought and Miss Stephens waited. At last, a boy named Dan raised his hand.

"It's wrong because God made him that way . . . and to make fun of George is to make fun of what God gave him."

"Yes, Dan," agreed Miss Stephens. "God chose to make some of us yellow-skinned, some red, some brown, and some white. We cannot choose our color. So it is foolish and wrong to be proud or ashamed of it. God gave each one what is best for him. But is one skin color better than another?"

"No," chorused the children, shaking their heads.

Miss Stephens held up her finger, "Listen and think about these words from the Bible, 'Who makes you different from someone else, and what do you have that was not given you? And if it has been given to you, why boast of it as if it were something you had gotten yourself?' (I Corinthians 4:7). And in another place God also tells us, 'In humility count others better than yourselves' (Philippians 2:3).

"Now we know what you did was wrong. But what will you do about it?" asked Miss Stephens. There was a long silence. Finally, a big boy named Sammy raised his hand.

"Miss Stephens . . . I, uh, I think we ought to tell George we're sorry." Sammy's face turned red. "I started calling him Brownie and I will tell him I'm sorry I did it."

So the problem was solved.

52

Billy Missionary

Dear Uncle Russ:

Mom is writing this letter for me to tell you about Chuck. He's the boy who moved into the house across the street last summer. He and I are good friends. We play together all the time.

Right after Chuck moved here, I asked him to go to vacation Bible school with me. At Bible school I sat with him and helped him — you know, so he wouldn't feel scared and funny 'cause he didn't know anybody.

Well, he liked it. But he didn't know any of the Bible stories. And he couldn't say any verses or sing Sunday school songs. I tried to teach him some songs and verses and stories. Then I had an idea. I asked Mom if we couldn't give Chuck one of our Bible-story books — we had two. She said I could, so I did. And I told Chuck to ask his dad to read a story every day with him like my dad does.

Now comes the best part — about Chuck, I mean. When Bible school was over, I asked him to go to Sunday school with me. And he went. Now he trusts Jesus like I do. Today he said that his dad and mom are going to come to church next Sunday. He thinks they will come every week. They didn't go to church before.

Mom and Dad and I pray for Chuck's dad and mother. We pray that they will believe in Jesus, too. I thought you'd like to hear about Chuck. When you talked with us at Sunday school, you told us we could be missionaries where we live. We could ask any kids who didn't go to Sunday school to go with us. I'm glad I asked Chuck.

I hope you will come and visit us again soon.

Billy

53

It Happened in India

Krishna Das sat in front of his plain little home. His head was bowed over a worn book. His dark eyes followed the queer, squiggly letters on the pages as he read aloud. Squatted around him, his neighbors listened quietly. Day after day the neighbors came to hear Krishna Das read from his book. "It is a good book," they said. "It speaks to our hearts."

For three years Krishna had read from the same book. Yet he was always glad to read it, and his neighbors never tired of listening. Again and again he read the little book through. It had brought happiness to him and to his neighbors. What they read in it had changed their lives.

After he heard what the book said, neighbor Jagannath Das had smashed the ugly idols he used to worship. Sebak Ram, a loud, rough man, stopped singing evil songs. Fisherman Gabardhan, who used to lie and cheat, became an honest man. And another neighbor who used to beat his wife began to treat her kindly. The village had become a different place since everyone listened to the words of the book.

"Krishna," his neighbors said one day, "we must find the Englishman who gave you this wonderful book. We must thank him for his good gift."

"But I don't know the man's name. I don't know where he lives," said Krishna. "See, here in the front of the book it only tells that the book was printed in Serampore."

"Then we will go to Serampore," said Jagannath Das,

Sebak Ram, and Gabardhan. "Perhaps the people there can tell us where to find the man. We will thank him for all the people of our village."

So the three neighbors set out for Serampore. There they found Mr. Ward, the Englishman who had given Krishna the little book — a Bengali New Testament. They thanked him over and over for the precious book that had brought happiness to their people.

"We trust in Jesus," the three men said. "We know He is the Saviour who came to give His life for our sin. We have broken the wood and stone gods we used to worship. Now we worship Jesus."

This good news made the missionary's eyes shine with tears of joy. He was glad he had had a New Testament in

the Bengali language to give to Krishna Das. *If only I could give God's Word to everyone in India who can read,* he thought. *Then many other boys and girls and men and women in the villages could have happy hearts, too.*

Prayer: Dear Lord Jesus, we thank You for Your Word which You have given us to tell about Yourself. We pray for all the children and men and women who do not have Your Word and do not know You. Send missionaries to give them Your Word. Help us to give money gladly to help them in their work. Amen.

54

The Secret Babu Couldn't Keep

Babu peeked around the big tree where he was hiding. Under another tree, not far away, sat a group of brown-skinned Indian children. In front of them a storyteller held up colored pictures and began telling a story. Babu held his ears shut tight. "I won't listen to the storyteller," he said to himself. "I'll just look at the pretty pictures."

But Babu's arms got tired holding his ears shut. One arm slipped down to rest and then the other. Before he knew it he was listening to the storyteller. She was telling a story, from a Holy Book, of a girl who had died and was made alive again. A great Holy Man simply took hold of the dead girl's hand and told her to live again. And she did.

Babu's dark eyes became big and round. "The holy Person who had power to make the dead girl live again is the Son of the God of heaven and earth," explained the woman. "It was a wonderful miracle for Him to give the girl life after she had died. But He will do something more wonderful for boys and girls like you who trust in Him. If you believe in Him, He will give you everlasting life. He can give you life that never ends — the kind of life you need to live forever in heaven."

I would like to have that kind of life, thought Babu, *But I don't understand how to get it.*

Soon the storytime was over. The boys and girls said goodbye to the storyteller and skipped home. Babu slipped from his hiding place and ran home, too. He didn't tell anyone where he had been, for his parents were Hindus. His father had commanded him, "Don't ever go to the children's class under the tree. That story-woman is a Christian. She will poison your mind."

So Babu had hidden behind a tree where he could watch the class. Father didn't say he couldn't *watch.* Then he had forgotten not to listen. *What if my mind has been poisoned? What will happen to me?* he wondered. He waited for something terrible to happen. When nothing did, he decided to watch the class again.

Babu hid behind the tree many times. As he listened to the stories from the Holy Book, he came to believe in the holy Person named Jesus. And he learned that he could ask Jesus to forgive his sins and to give him everlasting life.

"I may not tell my parents that I love the great Son of God," he told himself. "I'll have to keep it a secret."

137

But one day Babu's mother began to notice that he did not lie or steal anymore. Besides he was often helpful and kind. And many times, after he had been naughty, he even said he was sorry. "Something has happened to Babu," said his mother. "I wonder what it could be?"

Father, too, was surprised to find Babu more obedient and willing to work. *Something has happened to him,* thought Father. *I wonder what it could be?*

At last Mother and Father asked Babu, "You used to tell so many lies. You used to steal anything you could. And you were lazy and naughty. But now you are a different boy. What has happened to you?"

Babu looked frightened and hung his head. He curled his brown toes in the dust at the doorstep. Then he gulped, squared his shoulders bravely, and said, "Well, for many weeks I have been hiding behind the big tree and listening to the story-woman. And," he swallowed again, "And now I believe in the Holy Son of God who died on a cross for my sins. I asked Him to forgive my sins and to give me the life that doesn't end. . . . I meant to keep it a secret. But I guess if you belong to Jesus you can't keep it a secret."

55

My Sister

I've got a problem — my little sister Judy. You see, she thinks that I am pretty special. That's the trouble. She wants to follow me almost everywhere I go. If there is anything I don't need, it's a little sister following me around. But when I try to tell her, she doesn't understand. She laughs and jumps up and down. Then I have to laugh and can't scold her. So she just keeps following me.

Judy doesn't only follow me — she often tries to do what I do. It is like a game of follow-the-leader.

Near our house they are digging a deep ditch for some kind of pipes. The other day after school I was playing near it. I jumped across the ditch for fun. There was water in it because we had had lots of rain in the morning. All of a

sudden I heard a splash in the ditch like something big fell in. I looked to see what it was. And there was Judy. At least, what I could see — the feet and shoes — looked like Judy. She had followed me again!

I yelled for Mom and jumped into the ditch. Was I ever scared! I got Judy turned head up so she wouldn't drown. And Mom helped lift her out of the ditch. What a mess! Muddy water was dripping from her hair and clothes. But she gurgled and laughed. She said, "Danny jump. Judy jump, too."

We took Judy into the house, and Mom put her in the tub. In a few minutes she was shining clean again.

Mom looked as if she were thinking. She said, "You know, Judy thinks you're great. So she follows you and wants to be like you. But whom are you following, Danny? Whom do you want to be like?"

Then Mom wrote some words on the little chalkboard in our kitchen. She wrote, "Jesus said, *Follow me,*" and, *"I am the way, . . . no man cometh unto the Father but by me."* And we talked about how we needed to follow Jesus and how we would help teach Judy to trust in Him and follow Him, too.

Prayer: Dear heavenly Father, we thank You that the Lord Jesus is the way to heaven. We thank You that He calls boys and girls to follow Him. Help us to trust and obey him. Amen.

56

Beth's Wish

Beth pulled on her pajamas. She snatched up her favorite storybook and rushed to Daddy's chair, hopped up onto his knee, and squirmed to a comfortable position. Her eager fingers found the place in her book where she wanted Daddy to begin. And then Daddy began to read. She liked the way he read. Sometimes he read slowly and sometimes fast . . . or loud . . . or soft. He could roar like a lion or squeak like a mouse.

Mother had gone to a meeting, and Daddy had promised to read Beth a story before she went to bed. When Daddy finished one story Beth begged to hear more. So Daddy read another. And another. He liked to make his little girl happy.

But then Daddy smiled, "Young lady," he said in his "that's enough" voice, "to bed you go."

Beth took her book and slid off his knee.

"Daddy?"

"Umm-m?"

"Daddy, you know what? Before cousin Alice gets into bed she talks with God. She says God likes us to talk with Him."

Daddy didn't say anything. He tilted his head to one side and looked at Beth.

"Would you help me talk to God, too? I'd like to, but I don't know how."

Daddy looked a little sad. "I haven't talked with God for a long time, Beth. I don't know Him very well. But I can tell you what I used to say to Him when I was a boy."

He stood up. "Come, we'll kneel by your bed. We can say a prayer together."

Beth and Daddy knelt by her bed. Daddy told this prayer to Beth. Then they prayed,

> Now I lay me down to sleep;
> I pray Thee, Lord, my soul to keep.
> If I should live through other days,
> I pray Thee, Lord, to guide my ways. Amen.

Beth's eyes were shining. "Daddy, let's talk with God every night before I go to bed." She climbed into bed and snuggled under the covers.

Daddy walked slowly back to his chair and sat down. He looked thoughtful.

When Mother came home he told her how he and Beth had prayed. "You know, God put that wish into Beth's

heart to remind us that He wants us to teach her to know and love Him. But we can't do it unless we know and trust Him ourselves. Tomorrow we will begin to read the Bible. And on Sunday we will go to church."

So Daddy, Mother, and Beth read God's Word together and talked with Him every day that week. On Sunday morning Daddy and Mother walked to church with a happy Beth skipping between them. Daddy and Mother smiled at each other. Their eyes said, "Thank You, God, for Beth and for reminding us we need to know You and teach her about You."

57

Following the Rules

Why do we need rules? Couldn't we get along without them?

Look at Paul, Mary Lou, and Linda playing their game. Now imagine what would happen if they didn't follow the rules. Mary Lou might decide to move her piece ten blocks forward instead of five blocks as she was supposed to. Or Paul might not go back and start over when the rules said he should. Or Linda might take her turn whenever she wanted to. In no time at all they would be all mixed up and cross with each other.

It is no fun to play unless everyone plays fairly and follows the rules. Rules for games are made so we can enjoy playing together. Mary Lou, Paul, and Linda are having fun. They are obeying the rules of their game.

And Mother and Father are enjoying watching them play.

For what else besides games do we have rules? We have rules in our homes, at school, and we have the laws of our states and country. These help us to live together.

When Jesus lived on the earth He gave us some rules, too. He gave rules for those who believe in Him and belong to God's family. Where can we find His rules? Do you know what they are? Do you obey them? Here are a few of them:

Love your enemies.
Put God first in your life.
Do not worry because God knows what you need.
Treat others like you want them to treat you.
Forgive others as God forgives you.

Jesus said, "If any one hears these words and does them he is like a wise man."

Prayer: Dear Heavenly Father, we thank You for the rules and laws in our homes, schools, and country. Help us to obey them. And we thank You for the perfect rules You have given us in Your Word. Help us to follow them that we might please You and live happily in Your family. Amen.

58

No Room for Trash

Bill was sprawled on the sofa on his stomach. He lay quiet and still. But he wasn't asleep. His head was turned toward the edge of the sofa. And on the floor was an open comic book. It was more fun to read comic books than to study his lessons.

In the dining-room doorway stood Dad, watching Bill read. He scratched his head and frowned. He opened his mouth to say something to Bill, but then closed it again, shook his head, and walked away.

A few weeks later Bill brought home his first report card of the year. His low grades surprised him and made him feel ashamed. "I don't know why I get such poor marks," he grumbled as he handed his card to Dad.

Dad looked at the card. Bill bit a fingernail and waited for him to say something. But Dad just sat and looked

thoughtful. Then he said, "Bill, will you get the big basket from the basement? Fill it with the wood shavings and little scraps of wood by my workbench and bring it to me."

Bill was glad not to be scolded for his report card. He hurried to pile the basket full and high and bring it to his father.

"Now," said Dad, "Go pick up the best apples under our apple tree and put them into the basket."

"But how can I put apples into the basket?" asked Bill, looking puzzled. "It's full already."

"That's right," agreed Dad. "You can't put anything into a full basket, can you? . . . But that's what you have been trying to do. First you fill your mind full of stories from comic books. Then you try to put lessons and good things into it, too. And there isn't room for both!"

Bill stared at the basket full of wood scraps. Dad smiled and put his hand on Bill's shoulder. "You just have to decide what you want to put into your mind. What will you fill it with — good things that will help you, or foolish, poor, and even bad things?"

Bill grinned sheepishly, nodded, and made up his mind.

Prayer: Dear Father, we thank You for healthy minds, for teachers, and for schools. Help us to fill our minds, with the good things You have given us to learn and know. Amen.

59

Things Are Not Always What They Seem

It was almost lunch time at Maple Valley School and Helen couldn't find her lunch money. She felt around in her sweater pocket carefully. It wasn't there. It wasn't on her desk. She looked and looked but she couldn't find it anywhere.

Suddenly she thought, *Maybe I left it on my desk and someone took it during play period. That's what must have happened to it.*

Helen scowled, "Someone stole my lunch money," she announced loudly. And I bet I know who did it — it was Nicky."

Nicky's mouth opened in surprise. His face turned red as everyone looked at him. "I didn't take it," he stammered. "Honest, I didn't. I didn't even see your money."

"You were standing right by my desk when I came into the room," Helen said accusingly. "I bet you forgot your own lunch money, so you took mine."

Nicky shook his head. "No, no! I didn't! Cross my heart, I didn't."

But Helen wouldn't listen.

Poor Nicky felt miserable. The other children stared at him suspiciously. They wouldn't play with him and scarcely talked with him the rest of the day. And as he walked home from school two girls sang, "Nicky is a thief, Nicky is a thief!" The hurt showed in Nicky's eyes as he looked at them. And he hurried away.

Helen rushed home to tell her mother, "Nicky Steffen is a thief. He stole my lunch money off my desk today."

"Are you sure?" asked Mother. "Did you see him do it?"

"No-o-o. But he was standing at my desk when we came in from play period. And my money was gone. So I know he took it."

Mother looked concerned. "But he didn't take your money. You are accusing him wrongly. See, here it is on the table where you left it this morning."

Helen gasped and stared.

"I hope you didn't tell anyone else you thought Nicky had stolen."

"But I did," wailed Helen, looking ashamed. "What'll I do now?"

"What do you think you ought to do?"

How Helen hated to admit it when she was wrong! She bit her lip. "Guess I'll have to tell Nicky and the other kids what happened. And I'll have to tell Nicky I'm sorry

for what I thought and said. Mother, I'll simply die! I'll feel so silly and stupid."

Mother nodded. She understood. "But try to imagine how Nicky feels, and how do you think Jesus feels about such a wrong?"

Next time, decided Helen, helping herself to a glass of milk and a plump doughnut, *I won't be so quick to think or say someone has done wrong.*

60

The Village without a Bible

It was Sunday morning in Bala, a village in Wales, more than 150 years ago. Chattering happily, the village children hurried down the street on their way to Sunday school.

Quietly they entered the church. They took their places in the straight-backed pews. Soon Pastor Charles was ready to hear them say their memory verses. But imagine his surprise when not one of the boys or girls he called on knew his verse!

That's strange, he thought. *I'll call on little Mary next. She always knows her memory text.* Mary just squirmed in her seat and hung her head. She didn't know her verse either.

"Why didn't you learn your verse, Mary?" asked Pastor Charles kindly.

"Please, sir, the weather was very bad this week."

"Yes, it was," smiled the pastor. "But what did that have to do with not learning your verse?"

"Well, sir, we don't have Bibles of our own. And the only family who has one lives in the next village. It is a few miles over the hill, you know. I always walk to their house to look up my Bible verse. But Mama would not let me go this week because it rained every day."

The Rev. Charles was astonished. He looked around at the other children. "Does this mean that none of you have Bibles at home?"

The children nodded their heads.

"Welsh Bibles are scarce. They cost much money, sir," said an older boy.

The pastor nodded thoughtfully. "I didn't know that none of you had Bibles. We'll have to find a way for each of you to have a copy."

Rev. Charles had an idea. *I know what to do,* he thought to himself. *I'll go to London. I'll tell my friends about this. We'll start a Bible society to print Bibles in Welsh for these poor people.*

When Rev. Charles told his idea to his friends, one of them had a better suggestion. He said, "Why not start a Bible society for the world?"

That is what they did. They started the British and Foreign Bible Society. It sends out millions of Bibles to those who need them wherever they may be.

Prayer: Our Father in heaven, we thank You for our Bibles. We pray for the children who still do not have a copy of Your Word. Show us how we may help them. May we love Your Word and learn our memory verses gladly. Amen.

61

Dandelions

What's wrong? wondered Dad as he walked toward the house. Heidi is sitting quietly on the front steps. *She doesn't sit that still unless something is wrong. And she is never that quiet unless she is sick or unhappy.*

Dad strode up the walk in long steps and sat down beside Heidi.

"Hi, Heidi."

"Hi," answered Heidi unhappily.

"Well, I see you must have a big problem, Peanuts." (Peanuts was Dad's pet name for Heidi.) "Could I help?"

Heidi sighed. "Oh, Daddy, why do I do such stupid things?"

"What stupid things?"

"You know how I talk all the time? I'm such a blabbermouth."

"You do talk pretty much," smiled Dad. "But why does that make you sad today?"

Heidi stared at the tips of her shoes. "You know that new girl at school I told you about — Sharon?"

"Mm-hmm," murmured Dad.

"Well, we had a hard quiz today and she got 100. I guess I was jealous that she got 100 and I didn't. So I told everyone that I knew she'd cheated. But I didn't. Inside I didn't really think so. She's just smart. Anyway, some of the kids believed me. They called her names."

Dad raised his eyebrows.

"Before that I made fun of the different way she talks. And I guess I said some other things that were not nice or true. And now — now I feel bad inside about it."

Dad nodded. Heidi did have a big problem. Suddenly Dad had an idea. He stood up and looked across the road at the vacant lot. Near the road were many soft balls of dandelion seeds on long stems. He hurried across the street and carefully picked one of the seed balls. He walked back slowly, trying not to lose any of the fluffy seeds. Then he handed it to Heidi.

"Here, blow hard. See if you can blow all these seeds into the air."

Heidi took a deep breath and gave a big puff. Fluffy seeds scattered in all directions.

Dad sat down on the step again, and he and Heidi watched the seeds float away in the breeze.

"Now," said Dad, "I would like you to gather the seeds together again."

152

Heidi looked to see if he was joking. "Oh, Daddy! You can't gather dandelion seeds together again!"

"I know, Peanuts," agreed Father. "Anyone can scatter such seeds with a little puff of breath. But the strongest, wisest man cannot gather them up again. Just so, unkind words can easily be spoken. But you can't get them back or undo all the trouble they cause."

Heidi looked around. The seeds had vanished. "But what'll I do?"

"What do you think you ought to do?"

"I think I know what I ought to do — but it won't be easy. I think I should tell Sharon and the girls that I'm sorry for the things I said."

That is what Heidi did the very next day. Afterward, when she was tempted to speak unkindly about someone, she often remembered the dandelion seeds.

"Set a guard over my mouth, O Lord, keep watch over the door of my lips" (Psalm 141:3).

153